Melissa rode nearly wrapped over the back of her horse, fingers fisting the reins with Sassy's mane. She had chosen the bareback saddle so she could feel as one with the horse as possible.

The rhythm of hooves hitting earth numbed the noise in her brain. Noise that condemned her. She urged Sassy on to ride faster. She thought of Pegasus. She closed her eyes and imagined she was riding Pegasus. His wings spread wide and they lifted from the ground. The solid, heavy raising and lowering of his wings whipped the air.

Nothing matters when you're riding the winged horse. Traveling time and space. Your body wind-whipped. Rhythm piercing your soul.

She could barely breathe. The wind came and went from her lungs with the pounding of hooves and dark clouds breaking on one another. But she herself was not breathing.

Eyes still closed, she unclenched her right fist to press her palm against the soft furriness under Sassy's mane. Hot from riding hard, Sassy's coat began to stick to Melissa's hand as she held it there.

"Look out!" was the last thing she heard before she felt her body break.

LIGHT AT SUMMER'S END

Young Adult Fiction from Shaw

Absolutely Perfect Summer
Jeffrey Asher Nesbit

All the King's Horses
Jeffrey Asher Nesbit

Dark Is A Color
Fay S. Lapka

The Great Nothing Strikes Back
Jeffrey Asher Nesbit

Hoverlight
Fay S. Lapka

Light at Summer's End
Kimberly M. Ballard

Light at Summer's End

KIMBERLY M. BALLARD

Harold Shaw Publishers
Wheaton, Illinois

ISBN 0-87788-503-6

Cover design by Ron Kadrmas
Cover illustration © 1991 by Marcus Hamilton

Library of Congress Cataloging-in-Publication Data

Ballard, Kimberly M.
    Light at summer's end / Kimberly M. Ballard.
        p.   cm.
    Summary: Dumped off at a lady's house for the summer,
fourteen-year-old Melissa and her new guardian develop
a friendship as they work through the hurts of the past
and grapple with the issue of abortion.
    ISBN 0-87788-503-6
    [1. Friendship—Fiction. 2. Abortion—Fiction.] I. Title.
PZ7.B2116Li   1991   90-8950
[Fic]—dc20   CIP
                                         AC

---

99 98 97 96 95 94 93 92 91

10 9 8 7 6 5 4 3 2 1

for my twenty-seven million* brothers and sisters
who have been legally denied the right to live,
and for my brothers and sisters who know life.

It is up to us to stop the dying.
The first step is to know you are valuable.
This story is for you.

*An estimated 1½ million unborn babies have been aborted each year since January 22, 1973 (National Right to Life).

ONE

Vellie came out of the house looking for a breeze, a bowl of vanilla ice cream in her hands. She kept the screen door from slamming—she timed it instinctively and intercepted it a mere millimeter before it hit—without looking. Lowering herself into her "favorite" rocker (it was her only rocker), she managed to keep the ice cream in the bowl. She pulled the skirt of her pink flowered sundress up to her knees, and, though she was a true Southern lady, she reckoned it was all right not to have anything on her legs or feet on such a hot, Georgia afternoon. In fact, while no one questioned she was a lady, she had a balanced sense of not allowing what was *proper* to be out of proportion with what was *comfortable*.

She ate that first spoonful of ice cream as if she'd never tasted it before, savoring the cool sweetness with her eyes closed. As she swallowed, she looked out across the land. Her land. Nothing seemed to move out there in the sun. The longer grasses in the far-off meadow rippled occasionally. Though there had been little rain, humidity would come and settle thick as dumplings. And the sky seemed just as white.

This had been her husband Post's favorite time of year. She smiled to think of him. Actually, every time of year was his favorite. He had loved life and he loved to farm. He had been well educated and could have become anything. In fact his father had been a doctor and, as the only son, Post was expected to be likewise. But Post had other plans. He loved to be as involved in life as he could, whether it was with people, animals, or the land. He talked of working the land as being the highest form of healing for the human soul. Other farmers in the area looked at him as though he were a little loony. They farmed because that was what was theirs to do. Yes, they loved the land. Some were better businessmen than others. But for the most part they just shook their heads at Post's "phillisophical notions."

Vellie chuckled and put her empty ice cream bowl on the table an arm's length from her. She picked up the TV section of the newspaper she'd left out there from that morning, relaxed, and began to rock and fan herself. An unfelt breeze carried the faint scent of honeysuckle. And everything—even the birds—was quiet. The only sound was her wooden rocker rolling back and forth against the narrow wood planks of her immense front porch. The rough wood against wood rhythmically, repeatedly kinked through her body—so familiar it went unnoticed.

She heard the car come up the hill at the same time Jasper did. The old basset hound gave himself a partial push-up to bark and howl.

"All right, Jasper, I can see it comin'." Jasper was inspired to continue. As the canary yellow sedan barely came into view, Vellie shaded her brow with the newspaper and squinted. "Jasper, that's just Bill comin'." Jasper waddled to the edge of the porch and paid close attention going down the steps.

The car chewed the gravel and spewed dust clouds billowing behind it. Then it scrambled to a halt.

"Mornin' Mama." Bill accented his greeting with the slam of his car door. Vellie noticed a young girl in the back seat.

"Mornin'. Who you carryin'?"

"Ah, that's Melissa," Bill replied. Vellie raised her chin and looked suspiciously at her son. He always sounded a little too excited when trouble was close at hand. He opened the back door and a girl who looked about fourteen climbed out of the back seat. She held her head high and her body had a determined rigidness about it, but Vellie saw uncertainty, perhaps fear, in her eyes.

"Melissa, that there's Miss Evelyn Bagley. Most everbody calls her Miss Vellie. Mama, Melissa's Wanita's girl."

"Glad to meet you Melissa. Y'all come on up here outta that sun," Vellie called.

"It sure is hot." Bill finally knelt and gave Jasper some scrubbing behind the ears. Vellie watched Melissa eye the house, its width and height, the porch, and the steps as she came up. She rubbed the hand rail and then the post on her way as if she were a visiting princess in another queen's castle. Paying no attention to Vellie as she paraded past, she took a seat, a white wicker chair, at the round table near one end of the porch, almost with her back to Vellie.

"Are you thirsty, Melissa? I have some sweet tea in the refrigerator. I'd be glad to get you a glass." Vellie smiled, waiting.

Melissa sat like a statue, staring into the distant hills. Her thick dark hair shone auburn streaks in the sunlight that crept over the railing. She did not say a word.

Vellie's smile faded to concern. Puzzled, she looked at Bill who had also noticed the silence and looked up from his playing with the dog. He glanced first at Vellie and then at Melissa.

"Melissa, honey, Mama wants to know if you'd like some tea." He stood up and sauntered toward the porch. Jasper waddled alongside.

"No, thank you," she said politely. Stoically.

"All right, then," Vellie said quietly. "Son?"

"Yes, Mama, tea sounds lovely."

"I'll be right back." Vellie dropped the newspaper in her rocker behind her. She gave Bill a strong questioning, perhaps even slightly disapproving, look as she passed into the house.

Bill forced a toothy smile at her, more like a grimace. Then she disappeared.

"Melissa," he almost whispered so Vellie couldn't hear through the open windows, "I thought you were looking forward to coming to the country for the summer."

"*You* were looking forward," she accused. Her deep brown eyes were fierce. "*She* didn't even know I was coming. You're such a jerk." Melissa returned to her statue pose, having said her piece.

"Look—I'm sorry. I just didn't know what to tell her." Bill waited for a response. Any response. "It's gonna be okay, you'll see. It's gonna be fine for you to stay here."

Another silence.

Melissa continued to stare off in the distance.

"Melissa, please don't be difficult. You promised me you'd try to get along with her. Come on, what do you want from me?"

Vellie suddenly appeared through the screen door. "Maybe I should be asking that question of you," she said, in the motherly tone that seemed to prove she hears all. She carried the tray of three glasses of tea toward the table. Bill and Melissa glanced at her, interrupted. Again Melissa turned away.

Bill took the tray and set it gently on the table. Vellie took a glass off and handed it to Melissa. "It's mighty hot out here, Melissa. You don't have to drink it, but I brought it out in case you change your mind."

Bill grabbed a glass and plopped himself back in one of the chairs at the table, taking gulps of cold tea. "That's real good tea, Mama."

Vellie smiled at her son, pulling out a chair for herself. Bill quickly leaned up to gesture a gentlemanly help as she sat. "Never you mind, Bill." Vellie scooted her chair up herself, throwing a sideways grin at her first-born. "So what's your answer?" she asked playfully.

Bill looked at her blankly. "My answer?"

"What's this little visit all about?"

He chuckled, setting his glass on the table. "Good ol' Mama, always right to the point."

She waited for his reply.

"You know you'd make a great salesman, Mama. Always waiting for the other guy to talk hisself into a sale. Except I don't believe I want the competition."

"Himself," she corrected him, with the fluid reflex of a true English teacher. But her expression didn't change.

"Right. Okay, here's the beef. Wanita—you remember Wanita, don't you?"

She nodded. She glanced at Melissa who stirred slightly, twisting to see less of them and more of the fields.

"Well," Bill continued, "we need a trip away from everything right now . . ."

Melissa picked up her tea and took a sip. Vellie noticed but did not look in her direction. Vellie feigned attention to Bill, hearing the words, but it was Melissa she was tuned to, watching, as it were, her movement, trying to sense her feelings. Bill continued without distraction. "It's just that she's under a lot of pressure at work and we have this opportunity to go to Cancun, Mama . . ."

Melissa quietly rose from her chair and circled behind them toward the steps. Vellie's mind quickly raced through whether or not to stop her, show that she noticed, or just how to respond. She decided to let her go right now. Melissa continued walking away from the house, but she was still within Vellie's peripheral vision.

"So whataya say, Mama?" Bill pleaded.

"Say?"

"About Melissa's staying with you for the summer."

Vellie leaned back a little, taking in a breath. "I don't know, honey. She doesn't seem to want to be here."

"Nonsense! She's just hot and tired from the long drive. She's really not such a bad kid . . . where is she?" He stretched around suddenly to see off the porch.

Vellie motioned toward Melissa. She was almost as far as the pasture, fenced to keep in the ponies which were no longer there.

Vellie leaned forward. "Darlin', do you really think it's good for her to be out here for the entire summer?"

"Now Mama," Bill cajoled, placing the glass on the table and rising from his chair, "you know Wanita's been through a lot the last couple of years. I just wanna do somethin' nice for her. Take her out of all this for a while." He began to walk the length of the porch, choosing his words carefully. "It'll be good for Melissa, too. And you. I don't like you livin' out here alone. And Melissa needs somebody like you right now, too." He came up behind Vellie and put his hands on her shoulders, squeezing, pleading. "Please do this one thing for me, Mama. For Melissa's sake if not Wanita's."

Vellie looked again at Melissa who was approaching the far side of the pasture and would soon disappear over the hill near the creek. It had been a long time since she had had children in the house. She had just gotten to where she enjoyed not having another person besides herself to look after. She had looked forward to retiring. Thirty-five years of channeling teenage energy into the world of English and American literature was wonderfully rewarding. But now she was ready to enjoy her days full of what she called the three "r"s of retirement: reading, writing, and rocking. In fact, she had quite a number of projects on her desk that needed her attention. Now that time belonged to her, she wasn't sure if she wanted to give it up!

But there was something about this young girl that touched her. Perhaps it was the memory of herself as a young girl.

"What about what Melissa wants?" she challenged.

"She's fourteen, Mama. She doesn't know what she wants." He walked back behind his own chair and leaned on it.

"Besides, this isn't about what *she* wants, is it, Bill?"

"I wasn't thinking that."

"No, but it's true."

"Okay, Mama, it's true. I want some time alone with Wanita, and Melissa is nothing but trouble."

"She's her daughter."

"Yes, and she gets attention." He threw his arms in the air and turned to the porch railing.

"Bill." Vellie looked down, trying to put the right words together. "If you really love Wanita and want to make a life with her, you're gonna have to share her with Melissa. In fact, you're gonna have to make friends with Melissa. She is not a threat to you. She's a little girl who's lost her father. She's probably scared to death she's going to lose her mother, too."

Bill threw his head back and laughed. "Scared? Melissa? That girl ain't scared of nothin'. She's rude to me and downright mean to Wanita. I'm tired of her being around. I'm tired of seeing Wanita cry because of that girl."

Even when he was a little boy, Bill always tried to create a mood he thought would get him what he wanted. But it usually backfired, because he never quite learned when to quit. Nor did he have a firm handle on when extremes contradicted themselves and trapped him by revealing his true, and generally selfish, motives.

Vellie never could manage to keep from trying to make a point by playing on his melodrama. "So you thought you'd just dump her on good ol' Mama? A girl like that. Weren't you concerned she'd be too much for me? No, you have to think about having Wanita all to yourself instead of working things out with Melissa and helping Wanita work things out with her."

Bill huffed, "You do *not* understand—" He started pacing again.

Vellie wrapped both hands around her glass of tea. The ice had almost completely melted and the glass was covered with moisture. "Bill, sit down for a minute." She picked up her glass with one hand and wiped the cold sweat off with the other, spattering the wood slats below.

He paused for a moment as if debating, then took his chair.

Vellie continued. "I don't think you've handled this situation well. And I don't approve of you and Wanita just going off like this. But . . . I will keep Melissa—for *her* sake, not for you and not for Wanita."

Bill took her hands in his and kissed them. "Thank you, Mama. Y'all'll get along great, you'll see. Here, let me get her bags out. I got to be back in town to get Wanita from work. This is great, Mama!" He started down the stairs. The excitement stirred Jasper to barking and following Bill. "You'll see, Mama. Melissa's a great girl—really, she is."

Vellie shook her head at Bill. Looking toward the pasture, she saw nothing more than she did every day. Toward the Timmermanns' there were thick-trunked live oaks and maples, sprinkled with dogwood. Toward the creek were meadows of wild grains, which at one time boasted tobacco. Though she couldn't actually see the creek from the porch, she knew right where it cut through her property on its way to the Oconee River. She couldn't see Melissa either, but she knew Melissa was just beyond the edge of the hill.

"Here's all her stuff, Mama," Bill called as he stacked two big suitcases at the top of the steps and grabbed another overnight-type bag. "I'll just take 'em on up to Mark and Mike's old room—that's okay with you, isn't it?—and then I'll be on my way. C'mon Jasper."

The screen door squeaked, immediately followed by a *bang!* that shattered Vellie's thoughts and reminded her of former days. "Sorry Mama!" Bill's apology filtered down and out the door as he bounded upstairs. *At twelve or thirty-two,* she thought, *some things never change.* She smiled.

Vellie collected tea glasses back onto the tray to take in when she noticed Melissa wandering back toward the house. Vellie stood straight up, catching Melissa's eyes. Melissa stopped walking for a minute, then continued a little faster, looking down, playing with some weeds in her hand.

"Where's Bill?" Melissa asked, coming up the steps.

"Inside. Putting your things upstairs."

"So I'm staying." She sat down in Vellie's rocker.

"Disappointed?"

Melissa just shrugged her shoulders, looking out over the land.

Vellie leaned back against the table. "Melissa, you're welcome to stay with me." She stopped a minute, debating what to say. "I know you're angry. It's no fun getting left behind."

"Look, the way I see it, we're in sort of the same boat. I get dumped. And you get dumped on," Melissa said stiffly.

"I don't *feel* dumped on."

"Oh no?"

"No. I had a choice. And I chose to have you here for the summer. You have a choice."

"No way. I was dumped," Melissa countered.

"Maybe. But you can choose whether or not to like it—"

"I hate it."

"—or whether or not we become friends."

"Spare me the down-home routine, okay? I'm not a child. And I don't need you for a friend!" Melissa growled.

Bill and Jasper suddenly burst out the front door.

"Hey, women—" he drew the words out as if trying to scoop up a heavy load— "I hate to just run off like this, but you know how it goes." He went to Vellie, arms outstretched. "Thanks, Mama. I owe you one," he said softly, hugging her.

Vellie turned up her face for him to kiss her cheek. "When will you be back?"

"I dunno." He headed for Melissa. "But we'll be in touch, so don't you worry none." He leaned over to give Melissa a kiss, but she turned away. "Fine," he teased. "I give you a free summer's vacation in the country and this is how I'm treated. Well—" He took the steps down in two jumps and leapt to the car. "So long, you two. Have a great summer and keep smiling."

He roared off, leaving Jasper in the orange dust, barking.

Vellie took the tray inside. Melissa watched the pillows of dirt slowly rise like a rusty mist and spread thinner and thinner toward the sky.

Later that night, as the half moon shone brightly through her window, Vellie lay awake turning the events of the day over and over in her mind. Then, against all the familiar sounds in the darkness, she heard Melissa cry. Softly. She longed to go in and hold this angry, confused child, but she did not yet have the right to intrude.

TWO

The next morning, Melissa came downstairs to the kitchen. Vellie was nowhere to be seen. On the table were two bowls, spoons, and a box of homemade mueslix-type cereal. Orange peels on the counter confirmed that the orange juice in two glasses was fresh.

Vellie came in the back door, sweats on, carrying a grey pail full of milk. "Mornin'," she said. She set the pail down and closed the door.

"Hi," Melissa responded, surprised at her own eager tone. "This is real country, isn't it?"

Vellie chuckled, "Well, I'm not exactly sure what you mean. If it were real country, you'd be getting scrambled eggs, grits, biscuits, ham—with red-eye gravy, of course, and bacon and sausage, if there's company, along with this juice and milk. And coffee. Since it's just me these days, I've cut back a bit." She took a cup and dipped out milk into two glasses of ice. "Cereal's enough for me. If I'd known you were coming, I'd have prepared better. But that's not your fault."

"This is fine." Melissa took the glass of milk Vellie handed her.

"Did you sleep okay last night?" Vellie asked. They sat on opposite sides of the table.

"Yeah," Melissa answered, shrugging her shoulders.

"It's tough getting used to a new bed," Vellie empathized.

"Are those your horses on the other side of the creek?" Melissa asked. She filled her bowl and began to eat.

"No, those are Timmermanns'. They breed thoroughbreds and American saddle horses. Their son is ten or eleven and could sit a horse at three. You can't see their house from here—you can from the garden, though."

"Garden?"

"Mmm hmmm. Just follow that road out back there and you can't miss it."

Melissa nodded.

They ate much of their breakfast in silence. But silence has a way of bonding. And Vellie's attention to Melissa, to remembering what it was to be fourteen and living introspectively, helped create comfort in the silence.

"How come you don't have any horses?" Melissa tipped her bowl to spoon out the last bit of milk.

"I have Tavish. He's a good old horse. There's a small corral for him out behind the shed. In fact, that shed was really four stalls at one time. I just keep one now for Tavish. I took off the back so he can come and go as he likes. I let him roam in the pasture out yonder mostly, though."

Melissa took her bowl and glass and rinsed them off in the sink. "Do you ride him a lot?"

"When I go into town." Vellie took her bowl and glass to the sink, too. Melissa moved closer to the back door. Vellie continued, "It's about five miles, so it's good exercise for him. And if I go visiting, I sometimes ride him then—if it's not too far and if I'm in no real hurry. He can keep a fast pace, though. He's got energy! I'm the one who likes to move a bit slower."

"I think I'll go down to the river," Melissa said when Vellie paused. Melissa had been playing a little with the doorknob but not rudely. She seemed to be listening, but she rarely made eye contact with Vellie. And when she did, it was brief.

"Don't wait lunch for me; I may not be back by then."

"Well, then take something with you."

"No—," Melissa started to protest.

But Vellie had already grabbed a small paper bag off the counter and started dropping in a red-delicious apple and banana and other fruits from the basket by the refrigerator. "I'll have no argument. Just take these goodies with you so you'll have them when you get hungry. The creek water is clean enough if you get thirsty."

"Thank you," Melissa smiled, in spite of herself. She took the bag and left out the back door so she could walk by the shed to see Tavish.

Vellie swiftly tidied the kitchen and then went to her desk to tackle some work. She sighed as she sat and faced the stack. She'd just received the editor's comments on a few chapters she'd written for a new textbook of English literature for the tenth-grade level. And now before her lay the task of incorporating those changes as well as her own.

She sat staring at the stacks. They weren't big, but intimidating nonetheless. Her eyes wandered over to the corner table, almost adjacent to her desk. There were the members of her family, caught forever and framed. All different ages. Vacations. Her only daughter Carol's fourth Christmas—and first real doll. Bill and Mark on one of the Timmermanns' horses next door. Michael hanging from his knees on a tree branch.

She shook her head at Bill's seventh-grade graduation picture. At twelve he was still such a small guy. His hair was straight and brown, and he could never quite make it do anything in particular. He had an enchanting smile though and seemed to have lots of friends. He could really make things happen. Science and math were his favorite things, and he had gone on to Georgia Tech to study engineering. Now he sold software packages.

There was a picture of Mark at seven in his "Red Devils" football uniform in the same stance as his senior year in high school football picture. The only difference was that, at seven, he was simply a miniature of eighteen.

When Carol was born, Mark was two. From the moment they laid eyes on each other they were almost inseparable, until he went to Clemson on a football scholarship. They fought like normal kids growing up, but Mark always seemed to give in, mostly to get her off his back. Carol could be a real bossy kid. Post always called her "Princess" and she used that any chance she got.

Then there was Michael—such a fat baby. Vellie picked up a picture of all four children. Bill was ten years old, Mark was six, and Carol four. Michael was ten months old. She touched the image of his fat little body with her index finger. He was laughing. He made everyone laugh as he grew up. Always the center of attention, making up songs and rhymes. He liked to play jokes on people but wasn't vicious. Bill had played jokes growing up, too. But somehow he never learned when to quit. Michael had a better instinct for people.

Though she loved all her children, she and Michael had always been the closest. Maybe by the time he came Vellie was really feeling confident about mothering. She was more relaxed with him—Bill and Carol brought that up to her constantly, accusing her of spoiling him rotten. "You didn't let *us* do that when we were kids." That mostly came from Carol. Bill thought Carol *and* Michael were allowed to get away with everything. It seemed to Vellie that Bill should have handled things like that more maturely since he was the oldest—and ten years older than Michael, in fact. But Bill had such a temper. Such a chip on his shoulder.

Her eyes fell on a picture of Post and Bill when he was three. Billy, still rather bald, poor dear, was on his daddy's shoulders, holding fistfuls of hair. Post had been bouncing him around, giving him a camel ride. They were both laughing. Post must have been—she looked randomly at the wall, counting—forty-two. That's right. He was not quite forty when Bill was born.

A picture of Michael on his sixteenth birthday brought tears to her eyes. So handsome in his red sweater and black jeans, he was mounted on his new motorcycle. A black Yamaha.

She picked up her wedding picture. Post was so thin then. Even at thirty-eight. She had been only twenty-three. Her father had warned her not to marry such a *liberal*, especially one so much older. Vellie smiled. Post may have had his own way of thinking and doing things, but he was loyal and definite in his deep faith in God, in the land, and in his family. Liberal was the last thing her husband was.

When he died, she took consolation in his having lived a tremendously fulfilled life. There were no regrets. She had learned from him to do everything with full commitment and a sense of humor, and give her best to whatever she did. Those same qualities had somehow been born in Michael, too. And since Michael had been the only one still at home, they grew closer to fill the enormous gap of life Post had left behind.

She took a deep breath, setting the picture in its place.

THREE

When Melissa came back, it was nearly dark. Vellie was in the shed tending Tavish. Melissa found her and watched without saying anything.

As Vellie spread the clean, sweet-smelling straw around, she glanced behind her, subconsciously knowing she was being watched. "Hey there." She straightened up and wiped her forehead.

"Hi," Melissa responded shyly, seeming distant in thought, as if from a different world. "Can I help?"

"Sure." Vellie propped the fork up and stepped through the straw to get out of the stall.

"Show me what to do. I've never done—you know."

"No problem." Vellie showed her the chest where she kept Tavish's oats. "We just need to mix one cupful—the cup's in the chest—of that stuff in with his other grains in the trough. He eats mostly the grass out there, but I like to make sure he's getting a nutritious treat as well." She smiled.

With two hands, Melissa dug down into the oats and lifted the heaping cup. She carried it into the stall, found the trough, and poured it in. Tavish walked up, ears twitching. He startled Melissa, who backed suddenly out of the stall.

Vellie laughed. "Don't be afraid of the old guy. He's big, but he's a pussycat."

"Can I touch him?"

"Of course! Go on in there and give him a good hearty slap on the neck."

Melissa timidly approached him. He took his head out of the trough, turning to look at her, munching. As she came nearer, he stuck his nose back into the trough, disinterested. She barely touched his neck; then, as she got braver, she rubbed her hand along the neck, feeling every ridge, every muscle as he moved.

"I'm starved! How about some dinner? I've got a great stew waiting for us."

Melissa nodded her head and followed Vellie back to the house.

＊ ＊ ＊

The next morning Vellie woke Melissa up early enough to go with her to milk Belle, the cow, as Melissa had asked the night before. After watching Vellie a few minutes, Melissa took her place on the stool and shyly took a teat in each hand. She felt as if she were invading someone's privacy. Belle responded to the inexperienced stranger with quite a groaning "moo." But she squeezed and pulled firmly as Vellie instructed and succeeded in squirting fresh milk into the pail. The sound of the liquid sharply spraying against the sides of the almost empty pail gave her confidence to continue. A faint sweetness mixed with the smell of hay and early morning. The rhythm and ease she quickly developed, along with the warmth of Belle's body, created for her an intimacy she'd never felt before.

They did other chores together that morning: groomed Tavish, gathered the few eggs. Vellie showed her the garden. They shared lunch together in the kitchen, cooled by a small electric fan. Vellie explained that she enjoyed doing most of the chores herself, except that in the winter time she employed students to work the farm. And she had help year-round with the lawn maintenance and other major concerns.

Each of the days ahead would be full of similar chores. That evening, after milking Belle her second time, Vellie uncovered the cornbread she had made for the occasion. She told Melissa she hadn't made cornbread in a long time. But when she was a little girl, her grandmother would make cornbread just like this, thick and crumbly, to put in the fresh warm milk after dinner.

She filled Melissa's and her glasses two-thirds full of fresh, lukewarm milk, and showed Melissa how to break and crumble her cornbread into the liquid. Then they ate it, sweet and sopping, with a spoon.

FOUR

hat night, Vellie couldn't sleep. She thought she heard something and decided to take a walk.

The door to Melissa's room was cracked slightly. No light shone. Vellie gently pushed it open just enough to see in. Melissa faced the window and lay blanket-wrapped on her bed like a chrysalis, so very fragile. Vellie noticed her breathing was not the deep, restful breathing of sleep, but rather the pulsing of restless spurts. She was crying without a sound.

Such a mysterious young thing—sad, but likable. Whatever was tormenting her lay buried behind her dark face, dark eyes. Eyes that reflected hatred when Bill dropped her off. Eyes searching the opposite horizon to escape as he drove off. Eyes now full of tears here in her bed.

Vellie opened the door wider and tiptoed in. For a minute she stood by the bed deciding what to do. She knelt beside it, her face leveling the back of Melissa's head, and laid her hand gently on the bundle.

"Melissa," she whispered. The bundle stirred, stopped breathing. "Honey, what is it?"

Melissa didn't move. Instinctively, Vellie stroked Melissa's arm through the blanket.

"I know something is really hurting you. Won't you talk to me about it?"

"You don't know anything," Melissa said slowly, deliberately, catching her breath.

"I know you're not happy."

"Please go away and leave me alone," she whispered, her voice shaky. Vellie stayed a moment longer, then got the Kleenex box off the desk across the room and brought it to the night stand, on the side of the bed Melissa faced. Melissa pulled the covers over her head.

"When you're ready to talk," she said quietly, "I'll be ready to listen."

She closed the door gently and went downstairs to the kitchen. She emptied and refilled the kettle and then lit a match to the burner and raised the flame to her satisfaction. Grabbing her oversized mug and mason jar of powdered chocolate, she went out to the front porch table. *Midnight is so noisy,* she thought, wiggling comfortably into her rocker.

The full moon looked like a communion wafer on deep blue velvet cloth. She pictured her vicar leaning over her, placing the disc on her tongue as she knelt by the altar.

And the stars. Bright freckles flirting with the moon. She smiled at them. The earth had such a strange glow beneath it all. Like it didn't quite exist. All the colors were subdued, like they were sleeping, resting in the pulsating sounds of crickets, frogs, and other unseen creatures of the night.

She pressed her hand firmly on her arm, taking hold. Her cool, almost damp flesh warmed instantly to the heat of her palm.

Suddenly the screaming kettle startled her. She ran inside, pausing to keep the screen door from slamming, and grabbed the kettle off the flame. She also took down the trivet hanging beside the stove. Heading back to the porch, she thought of Melissa and slowed. Maybe Melissa would come down looking for her. She got another mug off the shelf just in case.

Back on the porch as she stirred in the powder, she heard the *shad shad shad* of Jasper on the dirt path coming from the shed where he slept. He struggled up the steps.

"Bet you're wondering why on earth I'm alive at this hour," she murmured, reaching over her chair's arm and fingering his thin velvet ear. He responded with a lick and then curled up in his place at the top of the steps.

She sipped the scalding liquid. What was she like at fourteen? It was hard to remember. Well, maybe not.

Her first year of high school, she was so awkward! She loved music and books. She used to spend hours reading fantasy stories, fairy tales, folk tales. She had always dreamed of one day teaching literature. Actually, if she were going to be honest about it, part of that dream was conceived out of rebellion against her father's expectations.

He had been mayor during her early teens and was known as quite a diplomat. He truly believed there were two ways of doing things—his way or the wrong way. But people still loved and respected him. Vellie was known then only as his daughter—his fourth daughter, in fact. She watched her three older sisters grow up and do everything right. They were ladies, proficient in dress, music, and speech. Vellie preferred to ride horses and climb trees. Part of that preference, she saw now, was a way to get his attention.

Another way to get his attention was to declare her decision to become a teacher. She was sixteen at the time. Her two older sisters were married—one to a doctor and one to a lawyer. The third sister was engaged to a missionary—dangerously close to rebellion in her father's political-success-oriented perspective. But the boy was highly intelligent and charmed the mayor to a blessing on their engagement. Vellie, on the other hand, wanted a career as a teacher. The night she informed her father of her intention, he was sitting in his navy blue, wing-back chair by the open hearth and lighting his pipe. She marched in from the kitchen and announced with all the courage she could muster, "Father, I have decided to become a teacher. And I would like to attend Agnes Scott College as soon as they accept my application."

He looked only with his eyes at her, head cocked, still sucking the flame from the match through the bowl of his pipe. Once it was lit to his satisfaction, he shook the flame out of the match with one hand and held his pipe away from his lips with the other. "I see," he replied, tossing the match into the fireplace. "And how do you plan to finance this venture?"

Her mind and heart raced. Did this mean he approved and truly wanted to know her plans? Or was he mocking her, thinking her a child who would grow out of this "phase"?

The aroma from the pipe tobacco and the snap of bark burning in the fireplace inspired her to answer enthusiastically, "Miss Josey said I could help her in the library after school and I'm already babysitting nearly every Saturday. And I can sell pies and cookies this summer at the fair."

Mayor Pritchard chuckled, "I see you have it all figured out."

Vellie smiled. "Yes sir."

"I reckon that's what you should do if you've a mind to." He picked up the evening paper from off the floor by the chair, opened it, shook it into place, and forgot she was there.

She took a deep breath and let her shoulders sag. She was victorious. But it had been a little too easy. And that was somehow disappointing.

FIVE

Upstairs, Melissa had gotten out of bed and
shuffled to the dresser mirror. She felt older
than she looked. Such a stupid little girl face
with red crybaby eyes. How stupid not to close the door
better. Next time she'd make sure it latched.

She had heard the tea kettle. And the scrape of the
rocker as Vellie rushed out of it back into the house.

*So that's her game. She's just waiting around down-
stairs for me to come—what, crawl into her lap like a big
baby? And why not, after that awful scene? I wish I'd
checked that door better. I'm not going down there. I'm
not playing this game.*

She sat on the bed and crossed her arms defiantly.

What does that old lady know anyway? Nothing. All she ever did was teach English. What does she know about real life?

She looked at the floor. Bill had shown her a picture of his family when he told her she would spend the summer here. Mostly so she could see what Vellie looked like. The picture had been taken in the winter time for Christmas. She remembered Vellie had on a brightly colored blouse with reds and burgundies, and a cobalt blue cardigan, buttoned. Her hands were in the pockets of her navy-blue corduroy skirt. Her short, black boots were laced up—sort of old fashioned but not. Her face . . . Melissa had looked at her face for a long time. Handsome, kind . . . overall attractive. Her hair was mostly silver, swept back off her face and then curled under at the neck, but she looked young. She seemed calm. Kind. Now having known her, Melissa recognized she had also seen a sparkle of fun in Vellie's eyes.

Melissa took a deep breath. She'd never met anyone like Vellie before. So why did she always find herself wanting to lash out at her? Melissa went over to the front window. The rest of the world was glowing with a silver sheen. She breathed in the warm, dewy grass and earth smells through her open window.

I wish I didn't know . . . Why, why did I ever read that letter? She went to the dresser and pulled open the middle drawer. Beneath tee shirts and underwear she found the small envelope. She opened it, sitting down on the bed. She took the letter out. Tears threatened to rush again. Without unfolding it, she slid it into its envelope and stuffed it back in the drawer. Suddenly she wanted to run, to get out.

She looked out the window again and wondered if Vellie were still on the porch. She'd just have to go down and see. She went to the bathroom, washed her face with cold water, and checked the mirror for puffy, red eyes. Yep, she had them all right. With a heavy sigh, she headed for the stairs. Though she didn't know why, she wanted to be with Vellie.

SIX

"Jasper." He lifted his head and looked at Vellie questioningly. Vellie continued without returning the look, "Do you think all those bugs are making that racket in their sleep?" He put his head back down, realizing she was really talking to herself at the expense of his name. "Or do you think they are awake? Like a sort of party. Or maybe they're communicating with the stars. No . . . I know! The stars' light and twinkle are reflections of the pulsating noise the bugs make. Look, look. See? It must be true! Isn't this wonderful, Jasper? We should do this more often." He gave a snort and turned away to rest his face on the other paw.

Vellie held the cup of hot chocolate up to her cheek. She thought of Post. How he had loved the full moon and summer nights. They would take long walks in the woods by the creek. One night, like many others, they walked until they reached the sharp turn. Post called it "The Elbow." The water was wider there to make the turn and about a foot and a half deep. He loved the river birches, so bright in the full moon. The banks were mossy and dry that summer, still warm from the day. They lay on their bellies, facing the creek.

"Silver water," Post said, sticking his long, tan finger in the moving water for a minute and taking it out again.

"Look at it." Vellie pointed down the creek. It wiggled and meandered between birches and pine, like a silver-glass ribbon. The trees glowed, too, but their leaves as well as the ground were dark.

Post leaned around to distract Vellie from her view and drew his wet finger around her face. "My little moon girl."

Vellie smiled at his boyishness. She had always found it hard to believe he was so much older. Somehow he had found the secret of staying young and playful. She leaned over and kissed him.

"Mmmmm. I want another one." He leaned back and puckered.

"Not in front of the moon," she whispered. "Besides, you don't deserve another one."

He opened his eyes. "Awww. I've been good. Besides, the moon doesn't care—he's busy swimming."

She squinted at him sideways. "Just one more. Then we have to get back to our children."

"Children," he said dismissively and pulled her down on top of himself and kissed her. Then he rolled the two of them, Vellie screaming and laughing, into the creek shouting, "Let's swim with the moon!"

The water was refreshing, but the air felt cooler than its 70 some degrees. They splashed around, Vellie trying to get out, Post keeping her in. "Post," she laughed, "Post, you are crazy! Let go of me!"

She managed to crawl out of the water but Post grabbed her ankle and she twisted over on her back, laughing and breathing heavily. He crawled up beside her, laughing and panting, too. He propped himself over her and wiped the hair from her face. "You're all wet, me lady."

"And why is that, darlin'?"

"Because you love me."

"Oh is that it? I thought it was because my silly husband's lost his mind."

"That, too," he agreed. He looked at her for a long time, and she lay there looking back. "You really are my little moon girl, you know. I can't imagine my life without you."

"Does that mean you love me, David Bagley?"

He crinkled his nose, "I wouldn't go that far."

"Oh you wouldn't?" She grabbed his sides.

"Okay, okay. I love you. I do indeed. David Bagley loves Evelyn Bagley."

"That's better. Now get off me! I'm freezing to death and we've got to get back to the house."

"Freezing?" He got up and gave a hand to help her up. "It's hot out here."

She leaned against him, arms around his waist. "Yeah, I know where it's hot," she retorted and started back for the house.

"Ooooh." He followed her. "You getting fresh with me, woman?"

She smiled at her own joke but didn't turn around. He followed close beside her, dancing as he walked. "How much?" He grabbed his wallet out of his back pocket, made a face at it because it was sopping wet, but continued, "For the whole night, I mean. I'd like to purchase a night with you."

She shook her head. Her pace was fast and they were nearing the house. "You're all wet, mister."

"That's okay, I'll dry."

"I dunno. You got any papers?"

"Papers? I got green papers with big numbers on 'em."

"You gotta do better'n that."

"Better?—Okay, how 'bout a marriage license? I got a marriage license."

"I guess that'll do."

He shouted and danced all around the yard. She had laughed at him then, and she laughed at the memory now. Then suddenly a darkness, like a shadow, clouded her thoughts. She looked at the moon. A mist out of nowhere seemed to smear it as it moved. "Will you forgive me, Post?" she whispered.

"Hi," Melissa said quietly. She had been standing behind the screen door, but now ventured out.

"Hi, darlin'." Vellie tried to sound cheery. "Come on out. I brought an extra cup in case you came down."

SEVEN

Melissa caught the door before it slammed and took the seat on Vellie's left, the same one she had sat in when she first arrived. She slipped into it carefully as if she were afraid that anything she touched might break. Or that if she didn't control every move she made she might bolt across the field. And she wanted to stay. For a little while.

"You like hot chocolate?" Vellie smiled, trying to put Melissa at ease.

"Sure." She tried to smile.

Vellie poured her a cup and refilled her own.

A few minutes of silence passed. Each in her own world, own thoughts. But it wasn't awkward, more a silence of respect and space. No demands. No expectations. Just hot chocolate, noise, and deep velvet full of bright lights.

"I think the moon is glad for our company," Vellie said in a loud whisper.

"Yes." Melissa smiled, still staring at the sky. The stars seemed enormous and much closer than she'd ever seen them. And the moonlight itself seemed almost warm. It was a different sky than the one she knew.

"I like the moon," Vellie continued. "I can always count on it to be there during my night."

Melissa looked at Vellie as if for the first time. "I thought the moon was the symbol of change."

"It is. But I can track those changes. Those changes are familiar to me. I know their patterns."

"What about 'new moon'?"

Vellie smiled out of one corner of her mouth and looked at Melissa sideways. "Okay, you got me. So I have to do without the moon one or two nights every month."

Melissa stared at the moon. "I like the moon, too. I'm not sure why it's the symbol of change. Like you said, it has a pattern. And no matter when you see it during its rotation, no matter what phase it's in, it always shows you the same side. No surprises."

Vellie listened with experienced ears, trying to decode the meaning behind Melissa's words. But the distance between what a young girl says and what she is really thinking can be dangerous waters. Vellie knew that. And so she chose her words carefully, words she hoped would help Melissa trust her.

"Don't you wonder about the other side?"

"No," Melissa said without expression.

"Not ever?"

Melissa cocked her head slightly but didn't reply.

"I sometimes wish the moon would show us the other side," Vellie continued, looking back at it. "I think seeing the dark side of the moon would help me understand the bright side better. Sometimes seeing other sides to something . . . or someone . . . helps bring you closer together."

Melissa barely heard her. Her mind wandered to that day when she was seven years old and had walked home from school early because she didn't feel well. It was only two blocks and when the teacher told her the line was busy at her apartment and she would have to stay in the infirmary, she decided to sneak out. She wore a key around her neck and went home alone all the time so she didn't think twice about it. After walking two blocks and climbing two flights of stairs she felt really hot and dizzy. She put her books down outside the door and took her mittens off—it was January. She had the talent and height for unlocking the bolt with the key and string still around her neck. With her foot, she slid her books and mittens into the apartment and to one side, took her jacket off, threw it on top, and kicked her shoes off while closing the door and then doublebolting it.

Her room was at the end of the hall and on her way she heard noises. She followed them to her mother's room. The door was open slightly and Melissa pushed it carefully so she could see in better. She saw her mother and some man in bed together. She jumped back, frightened, into the shadow of the hall. Her heart pounded and she felt paralyzed. She sort of knew what they were doing but had never seen it before. It made her feel dirty but she didn't know why. Putting her hands over her ears, she trotted quietly to her room, closed the door without a sound, and climbed in bed, shivering from the fever and the fright.

"Are you chilly, darlin'?"

Melissa jumped. She had started rubbing her arms.

"I'm sorry, did I startle you?" Vellie instinctively reached for her arm but Melissa avoided it.

"A little, I guess."

"Must've been some trip you took."

Melissa forced a smile. Then she noticed two hooks hanging from the ceiling behind Vellie at the other end of the porch. "Are those for a porch swing?"

Vellie turned her head unnecessarily to see where Melissa pointed. She nodded.

"What happened to it?"

"We took it down several years ago." Vellie had not yet turned her gaze away from where the swing should have been.

"How come?"

"Oh, no real reason. Just needed a change, really. It was getting old and I was afraid those hooks might not hold it up there forever." For a moment Vellie almost saw her sons Michael and Mark playing on it as small children.

Vellie stretched her back and rose, grabbing the kettle.

"Where you going?" Melissa surprised herself with the question, but Vellie seemed to take it in stride.

"To get some more water a'boilin'." Vellie mocked her own Southern expression, opened the door, and turned back to face Melissa. "We 'done drunk' this kettle dry, Missy." She let the door slam behind her for fun.

Melissa looked out over the fields. No one had ever called her "Missy" before. She sort of liked it—from Vellie. But probably not if Bill or just anybody called her that.

"Should be ready directly," Vellie said, coming back through the door, closing it gently this time. She took her place in the rocker.

They drifted back into silence again. After a few minutes, the kettle whistle blew. Jasper rolled over with a huff.

"I'll get it." Melissa was through the door instantly.

She reappeared with the kettle and refilled the cups while Vellie spooned in more chocolate.

"What have you found to do during the day?" Vellie asked.

"Mostly I go down to the pasture where the horses are."

"You like horses?"

"Yes."

"You like to ride?"

"I've never been riding."

"Really?"

"They don't have horses in the city."

"Right." Vellie chuckled at herself. "That's why you seemed so timid around Tavish. Well, would you like to go riding sometime?"

"Yes, I guess so."

"Sounds a little scary, doesn't it?"

Melissa shrugged.

"You'll catch on in no time. You've already made friends with Tavish and the Timmermann horses and that's half the battle."

Melissa smiled, "Well, I haven't actually gone inside the fence with them. Mostly I sit by the river and watch."

"All day?"

"Well, I take a book with me."

"Oh. You like to read."

"Yes." Melissa talked faster with excitement. "And I found a whole lot of great books in that other room upstairs—" She stopped short, embarrassed.

"What?" Vellie's face reflected Melissa's.

"I'm sorry," Melissa said seriously, "I should have asked first. And I shouldn't have been snooping around the house." She hung her head.

Vellie smiled, leaned over to Melissa, and drew her finger along Melissa's face, lifting her chin. "My house is your house, darlin'. You may go exploring. You may borrow books. I know you won't hurt them," she said gently. She sat back up, continuing, trying to lighten the mood, "You may visit horses! You may drink hot chocolate!"

Melissa couldn't say anything. She just sipped from her cup.

Vellie sensed her discomfort. "Tired yet?"

Melissa shook her head.

Vellie leaned in and whispered loudly, "We'll prob'ly be dead tomorrow."

Melissa smiled.

"We could declare it a national holiday—Day of Sleep—and just sleep all day. Sound good?"

"Why not?" Melissa finally joined in.

"So what did you find to read?"

"Till We Have Faces."

"C.S. Lewis. What a great writer. Do you like the story?"

"Very much. I'm not very far in yet. I'm at the part where Orual goes to see the younger sister Psyche the night before she is to be sacrificed to the gods because of her beauty. She told Orual that men are cruel, cowards, and liars because they don't know the difference between good and bad any longer. Psyche even pities them."

"Mmmmm." Vellie nodded.

"I don't. People don't know right from wrong or good from bad because they're just stupid. If they'd think about somebody else for two seconds instead of just doing what *they* want—" Melissa stopped, suddenly feeling self-conscious. Vellie didn't say anything, but she looked at Melissa with concern.

Melissa felt the need to redeem herself and lighten the topic. "Anyway, we studied Greek myths in school this year and I really enjoy them."

"They're some of the most imaginative stories in all of literature." Vellie matched her tone.

"Yes. I think the story of Pegasus is my favorite," Melissa continued, almost falsely.

"He is very grand and noble, I agree. Do you remember how the poets say he was born?"

Melissa nodded. "From the blood of the Gorgon Medussa when Perseus cut her head off."

"Mmmmm. The myths, at least my favorite ones, have a wonderful way of showing how something good or beautiful can come from something frightening. Or horrible."

Melissa showed no response.

"Bill tells me you'll be in the tenth grade next year."

Melissa's face clouded over. Hearing Bill's name reminded her of her mother. And that letter to Bill she'd found before the mailman had come. All the things her mother had said in it.

"You miss your mother?" Vellie volunteered.

"No. I don't care if I ever see her again."

"Melissa."

"It's true. She doesn't care anything about me, so why should I care about her?"

"What makes you think she doesn't care?"

Melissa looked at Vellie with the same "get real" look her students would sometimes give her.

"She left me here, didn't she?"

"Don't you like it here?"

"That's not the point. The point is, she didn't want me anywhere near her."

"Doing something *for* herself doesn't automatically mean it's *against* you," Vellie explained.

Melissa looked at her blankly, then finally said, "Forget it. It's too complicated to get into." Melissa sat back in her chair.

Vellie let a few minutes pass and then asked, "Do you have any brothers or sisters?"

"Two older brothers. Half brothers, really. I don't know them real well. One is living with his father, and the other is married and lives somewhere else. My father—his name is Carlos—has three other kids besides me—two girls and a boy. They're older, too. I don't ever see them. They lived with us off and on when I was a baby."

Vellie raised her eyebrows. *What a complicated, dysfunctional family,* she thought. *How did Bill ever find Wanita in the first place?* Of course, she knew the facts. Wanita worked in the accounting office where Bill worked. She had started working there about a year ago. Three months later, they had started dating. But Vellie had yet to meet her. From listening to Bill she gathered that Wanita had a lot of energy and was primarily interested in having a great time. And probably, though Bill would never see it, she was quite self-centered. She also struck Vellie as being the kind of woman who gets bored quickly. Melissa had confirmed that for her, mentioning at least two other men in Wanita's life.

"Where's your father now?" Vellie broke her own silence.

"I don't know. Look . . . " Melissa was suddenly irritated and close to tears again. "I'm tired now. I'm gonna go back to bed." She took her mug and headed for the door.

Vellie twisted in her rocker to face her. "Melissa."

Melissa stopped.

"I'm glad you're here. Thanks for watching the moon with me tonight."

Melissa looked away, then disappeared inside the house without a word.

Vellie took a sip of her now lukewarm chocolate. She made a face and smacked her lips. Jasper looked at her, waiting for her to speak.

"Yes, Jasper, you may return to the shed. Mama's gonna be good and go to bed, too."

Jasper rose, waddled down the stairs, and crept back around the side of the house. Vellie sighed. Picking up her mug, kettle, and trivet, she let the door slam behind her as she re-entered the house.

EIGHT

Finally the morning came when Vellie and Melissa walked over to the Timmermanns' stables to begin Melissa's horseback riding lessons. Vellie stopped an exercise boy to ask where Tim was. He pointed to the building behind him.

They found Tim pounding a horseshoe into the back hoof of a great grey horse.

"Tim!" Vellie had to shout over the piercing metal hitting metal.

Tim looked up and smiled, setting the hoof back down to the ground. "Well g'mornin', Miss Vellie."

"Tim, I'd like you to meet my guest for the summer, Melissa . . ."

"Jones," Melissa filled in for her.

"Melissa, this is my neighbor Tim Timmermann."

"Mighty nice to meet ya, Melissa." Tim held out his chubby palm and Melissa shook it.

He was tall enough that the chub didn't appear fat, but he looked like a little boy giant to Melissa. He had a round face and his eyes disappeared when he smiled. He wore cowboy boots and his jeans were faded at the knees. His tee shirt was white with a cigarette pack rolled up in the sleeve in a way that made them sit on his shoulder. He reminded her of the guys who hung out at her apartment—all except the cowboy boots.

His appearance seemed odd to her. She realized she was expecting him to look like the men in those fox-hunting pictures with tight little hats, pants that bulged at the thighs and slick black boots, although she didn't really know why.

"Over there's my son Sammy." Tim pointed to a corral where a little skinny boy was riding a horse at a trot around the ring. The horse was almost black and his head was cocked like a carousel horse. His tail stuck up and the hair flowed back and rippled like a water fountain. His shoulders were enormous, seemingly more so because of the size of Sammy.

"He's riding Torture, one of our American Saddle Horses. We have two dams that should foal this summer, thanks to that stallion."

"He's beautiful," Melissa said under her breath.

"Do you ride?" Tim asked Melissa.

"No—" She looked at Vellie.

"That's why we came over today, Tim. We were hoping you or maybe Sammy could work in a few riding lessons for Melissa. She's spent time over by the creek making friends with some of your horses."

"Ah. Well, let's see. I think I may be available. If you've been on that side of the property you've probably met Sassy. She's a good ol' horse we use when working with the thoroughbreds. She's a decent mount with a nice jump but we don't show her. What do you think?"

"Sounds fine," Melissa answered.

"Good. Tell you what—if you like her, I'll let you take her back with you to Miss Vellie's and you can keep her there."

"Thank you."

Melissa looked around the corridors of stalls from one building to the next. And then several buildings alongside. The place seemed enormous, especially compared to Vellie's one barn with the four stalls. Everything was buzzing—men as well as women saddling horses, riding horses, setting up jumps in different places outside.

Tim took them to a stall in another section. The barns, he explained, were sectioned off according to types of horses and those horses that belonged to the ranch and those that were boarded and trained there. The area they were entering kept the mounts used while training the thoroughbreds.

And then they reached Sassy's stall. She was a small mare compared to the horses in training. Her light brown coat was shiny. She seemed calm and friendly, but Tim warned she was spirited. She wouldn't give a dull ride.

Melissa loved the sounds of boots and hooves swishing in the straw and the pounding of the horses' hooves cantering around barrels and over jumps in the corrals nearby. Their snorting reached her deep inside. She breathed in the smells of animal flesh mixed with hay and dust and decided that she must have equestrian blood in her veins.

"Well, shall we saddle up?" Tim asked, smiling. Melissa nodded and Tim invited Vellie to join them.

"No, I'll head back to the house. Y'all have a good time. Now don't overdo it on this first day. Tim, you remember she's never been on a horse before; she's likely to get real sore."

"That's part of the fun, Miss Vellie. Now don't you worry none, I'll take real good care of your girl. She'll be a jockey in no time. Right, honey?"

Melissa nodded her head, smiling.

"Okay, then, I'll see you later this afternoon." Vellie smiled at Melissa who looked both thrilled and terrified.

"By the way, Tim, is Tracie here today?" Vellie asked.

Tim looked at his watch, "She should be back at the house now. Give it a try. She'd love to see you."

"Great. See y'all later!" Vellie waved over her head as she turned back toward the entry. She could hear Tim starting in with all the vocabulary of tack and riding. As she neared the doors, she turned to watch Tim and

Melissa. Tim was such a big man, but kind. And he had a marvelous sense of humor and spirit of fun.

He was listing his expectations, rules really, of Melissa before she would be allowed to mount. He sounded like he had when Michael got his motorcycle. Post had died two years before, and Tim had taken an uncle role in Michael's life. Vellie had discussed the motorcycle with Tim before she conceded to give it as a gift for Michael's sixteenth birthday.

Vellie took a deep breath and continued on her way.

As she approached the modern, three-story home, much too big for their family in Vellie's opinion, Tracie was just arriving in her white and gold-chromed Volvo. Tracie and Tim had been married for almost six years before Sammy was born. She was much too busy for children, she had told him. But Tim had wanted so much to have children grow up and learn to ride and show alongside him. Vellie didn't know how they'd met but remembered that when she'd first met Tracie eighteen years ago, she had thought they were an unlikely couple. On the other hand, they both had the same sense of humor and fun. Tracie was simply a well-to-do, princess-like city girl and Tim was a good-ol'-boy horse breeder and trainer. But Tracie loved the animals and the shows and had become quite an equestrian herself. Still, she determined to make her biweekly trip into the Big City for her own sanity.

"Miss Vellie!" Tracie called with energy. Opening the back door to the car, she grabbed two grocery bags and bumped it shut with her hip. "How nice to see you!

Please come in for a glass of ice tea." They ascended the stairs to the front door. "I get so thirsty when I'm out running around."

"Let me take one of those bags for you, Tracie." Vellie opened the door and they went inside.

"No, no. This way I'm balanced. And Nelli ought to be coming through the door any minute—"

And Nelli did, as if summoned. She was their Jamaican cook who was married to a trainer who worked with Tim. Tim had found them at one of the shows and was impressed with Jonson's rapport with the horses. They both agreed to come work for the Timmermanns and live in the third floor of the house. There was a separate entrance and stairway out back so they could come and go with privacy.

Nelli took the bags, greeting both Tracie and Vellie. "Nelli, please make some ice tea for us. We'll be out in the sun room." Nelli nodded and disappeared.

The sun room was on the east side of the house and was screened in on three sides. They could see most of the exercise areas, and about a half mile away, lay the track. The parlor on the other side of the house looked out into an open pasture and then woods, but this time of day was much hotter.

"I love getting groceries first thing in the morning," Tracie said, sitting in one of the wicker rockers, putting her feet up on the little wicker chest that served as a coffee table. All the furniture was white wicker and so much more delicate than the porch furniture at Vellie's. It was also considerably newer.

"Do you still go every morning?"

Tracie nodded. "I like the routine. And that way I only pick up a couple of bags—whatever's needed that day. Any real grocery shopping is done by Nelli. She makes sure Tim, Sammy, and Jonson are well fed. The others bring their lunches. So what brings you over?" She had a knack for hopping subjects like flies on watermelon.

"Bill's girlfriend's daughter is staying with me this summer. Her name's Melissa. I thought she'd like to learn how to ride so I brought her over to Tim. There they are." She pointed toward the barn where Tim and Melissa each came out slowly on a horse. Melissa was sitting rigidly and Tim was laughing at her, trying to get her to relax.

"She's very pretty," Tracie said, leaning up to see better.

Nelli came out with iced tea and fresh fruit cubed and in a white china bowl with a gold rim.

"Thank you, Nelli." Vellie took her glass of tea in both hands. It wasn't unendurably hot that day, but the cool wetness was refreshing. She was thirstier than she thought.

"Yes, thank you, Nelli." Tracie took her glass and leaned back in the chair, putting her feet back up on the table.

"Yes, she is very pretty."

"How old is she?" asked Tracie.

"I believe she's fourteen. But she'll be entering tenth grade."

"Right down your alley."

"I don't know. Teaching them is different than living with them."

"I guess that's right. Fourteen. What a difficult age. Especially these days. So how come she's with you this summer?"

Tracie had a fascination with simply knowing everything about everything. And even though the town was small and geographically distant, news had a way of reaching everyone once it hit Tracie. She was harmless, though. But Vellie preferred to protect herself and her family by not telling everything she knew.

"Oh, her mother thought it would be good for Melissa to have a change of scenery. You know, get away from the city for a couple of months."

"How does she like it so far? Bored stiff?"

"Actually," Vellie replied, seeing Tracie smile, "she's getting along just fine. She's even gotten up early enough to help milk the cow a couple of mornings. She really enjoys the horses, though." Vellie stared off. She could still see Tim and Melissa as they rode slowly down the path away from the house and toward the track. She remembered when she was that age and felt more at home in the country with all the animals than she did in town where she lived. There was something just in the being with an animal . . . a camaraderie, a quiet, private language and world so apart from any problems at home.

"I never really liked horses." Tracie crinkled her nose. "They were big, smelly creatures and I guess I was

60

always a little afraid of them. Until I met Tim, of course. He has a way of changing your mind about things."

"Yes, I know." She remembered Tim gently convincing her to get Michael the motorcycle. Michael had begged her for months. It was the only thing he wanted. She had discussed it with Mark and Bill and they seemed to think he was mature enough to handle the responsibility. Vellie was skeptical, not about his maturity, but about the machine. Her uncle had had a motorcycle accident when she was a little girl. He had recovered, but it had scared her so much that she was wary of her son owning such a dangerous vehicle. Mark reassured her that the machines were much safer than they had been. And Michael promised to wear a helmet and be very careful. Vellie also made him promise to ride it only on their land and dirt roads. He had given her a kiss and told her not to worry; he wasn't a stupid kid.

She still tried to dissuade him, but he begged her to at least talk to Tim before she made up her mind. Tim thought it would be good for Michael and agreed to Vellie's rules, believing, she knew, that she would mellow with time and Michael's maturity. Tim had ridden dirt bikes in competition when he was a younger man and she felt confident in his teaching Michael to ride with the same alertness and reflex—though, she hoped, not with the same aggression and competitiveness.

The morning of Michael's birthday, Bill drove up with the Yamaha chained on a flat trailer hitched to his car. Michael was ecstatic! He drove it on the property most of the day, taking everyone for a ride. Even Vellie agreed to ride it with him—but only to the edge of the property, which, from the house to the property line, was close to a mile and a half. Seeing him and Tim working together, as well as riding it herself, helped her relax about it some. For a moment she saw Tim with Michael on the cycle instead of Melissa on horseback. She took a deep breath. "Well, Tracie, I need to be running. The morning's about gone and I have things to do."

"Oh don't rush off. You hardly come over any more. I miss your visits," Tracie complained.

Vellie smiled, rising. "I appreciate that. With Melissa here and learning to ride, perhaps I'll see more of you."

"I'd like that." Tracie followed Vellie out to the front of the house and watched her walk down the lane.

NINE

When Melissa got home that afternoon she entered a house brimming with warm, delicious cooking aromas. Vellie was baking chicken and was at the moment creaming corn at the table.

"Hey," Melissa said, breathless but smiling. She walked like she had a barrel between her legs. Vellie chuckled.

"I told you you'd be sore."

"But it was wonderful. And Tim just cleaned out a stall in the barn for Sassy."

"I saw you both when you got here."

"He's so nice. And really funny. I like him."

"Well, tell me how it went."

Melissa lowered herself gingerly into a chair. "First we rode down to the track—they have a whole race track. And we watched one of the thoroughbreds run. They time it and everything. It was great. Then we rode some more—oh, just all over the place. He showed me where your property and his property connect. And he told me you used to have ponies in that pasture near the creek."

"We did. Post kept them for the summer carnival so the town kids could ride them in a circle, you know. They were beautiful, all five of them."

"What happened to them?"

"Didn't Tim tell you?"

"He said he wasn't sure."

"Well, after Post died, Bill and Mark were off at college and didn't want to bother with them on their summer breaks and Michael was really too young—actually, he was no more interested than his brothers. So we sold three of them. Two of them live with my sister. At the time she had two little grandchildren and she kept the ponies for them to ride when they visited."

Vellie picked up another ear and began to shuck it. "So what else did you do?"

"We watched Sammy exercise Torture. He's really good. I can't believe he's only ten. He seems so much older."

Vellie looked at Melissa and smiled. "Sammy's growing up in an adult world. No brothers or sisters. Tends to change the whole definition of childhood."

Melissa looked at Vellie for a moment, then down at her fingers. It was almost like Vellie was talking about her. Vellie seemed to know more than it was possible for her to know. What *did* she know? Melissa didn't know anyone who listened—or talked—quite like Vellie did.

Melissa tried to think of something to say. "How come there aren't any other children? Seems like Tim likes kids. And he and Sammy have a great time."

Vellie breathed deeply and looked absently across the room in thought. "Tim does love kids. He was like a big brother, or an uncle, to my younger kids. And I used to bring my students out here once a year for a year-end party and he always had them over and let them ride. I don't know why Sammy's an only child."

She thought for a minute. "Tracie's not a domestic type. She doesn't like kids very much, from what I gathered. She doesn't *dis*like them; I just get the impression she didn't really want a family." She glanced at Melissa, debating whether to voice her next thought, then said, "Maybe Sammy was a surprise."

Melissa returned a sharp questioning look. Vellie wondered what she was asking. But there was only silence. Melissa turned back to her hands.

"Or," Vellie broke the silence quietly, "Maybe they planned carefully just to have one child. To have Sammy."

Melissa didn't respond.

Vellie took the pot of creamed corn to the stove and began to tidy up the table covered with husks. Then, bringing the tone back to normal, she asked, "So you and Tim moved Sassy in okay?"

"Yes. We brought over grooming stuff, whatever you don't already have. He showed me how to do *every*thing.

He's so detailed. Tomorrow he said we could ride all the way to town."

Vellie stopped and looked at Melissa. "Are you up to that? That's quite a ride—look how sore you are now. Tomorrow morning your body will be sore in places you never knew you had before."

"Tim says it's important to keep working the kinks out or I'll *really* get stiff."

"Tim's a sadist." Vellie smiled.

"I think I'm really going to like horseback riding. I always wanted a horse. Tim said Sassy's mine for the summer. *Mine.* Isn't that great?"

"Sure is, darlin'." Vellie smiled. It was wonderful to see Melissa beginning to enjoy herself. Something inside was beginning to come alive and Vellie was warmed to watch it grow.

TEN

Evenings in the summer sometimes stir the scent of earth to breeze throughout an open house before a cleansing rain. A storm was lingering in the distant eastern sky. It was too early to tell if it would make it to the farm, or, if it did, how strong it might be.

Vellie was in the kitchen baking. Melissa was upstairs taking a shower, having spent the afternoon riding. The last few days Melissa had spent most of her time at Timmermanns'. Tim had told Vellie that Melissa was a natural at riding. She'd be ready for more stunts soon.

When she came down, she was toweling her thick, black hair.

"Your hair is gorgeous," Vellie said, watching Melissa scrub it with the towel.

"Thanks," she said, wrapping the towel around her head like a turban. "Anything I can do to help?"

"Sure. I just finished this bag of flour—will you get another one from the pantry? I believe it's near the back, fourth shelf down, on the right."

Melissa obeyed and they continued to work together in conversation. Melissa began putting the cookies on a cookie sheet and Vellie continued on with her pies.

"So where are Bill and Wanita spending their vacation? Bill mentioned it but I've forgotten."

Melissa stiffened some. "They've gone to Mexico, to Cancun."

Vellie watched Melissa for a moment, noting the change, the stiffness. "Melissa, you've been here, what, three weeks?"

"Something like that."

"You seem to enjoy being here."

"Very much."

"We've become pretty good friends, I think."

Melissa nodded, spooning the dough onto a cookie sheet.

"Well, as your friend, I'm concerned about you."

Melissa stopped her work, leaned with both hands onto the counter and twisted her face to look at Vellie, as if bracing herself. "Okay," she managed. "What are you concerned about?"

Vellie leaned back against the table, hands on the counter at either side of her hips. She chose her words very carefully. "I don't think you're sleeping very well," Vellie's voice trailed. She looked at her hand and began picking idly at the bits of dough stuck to her fingers. She took a deep breath and continued, "We both know I've heard you cry several different nights. And I know something is really troubling you. At first I thought maybe you were homesick. But I don't think that's it."

"What *do* you think?" Melissa ventured with a hint of accusation.

Vellie thought a moment, then replied cautiously, "I don't know. I—"

"Why do you think you have to know?" Melissa interrupted.

"Because I care about you."

"Why?"

"Because I do. Melissa, you're a beautiful, intelligent, lovely young lady and I want to be your friend."

Melissa threw her head back and took in a deep breath, fighting back the tears. "Trust me, you really *don't* want to be my friend."

"But I do."

Melissa shook her head and crossed her arms, squeezing her own shoulders. She sounded almost desperate. "No. And you can't help me."

"How do you know?" Vellie asked sincerely.

"Because I know, all right? Just leave me alone. I like you. I like being here, but please just leave me alone." She continued to breathe deeply to fight back the tears.

Vellie watched her for a minute, then said quietly, "I'm afraid I can't do that. I'm sorry if it seems like I'm prying, but—"

"That's exactly what it is."

"But . . . " Vellie raised her voice to drown out the interruption, then continued quietly again, "I care about you—you can't control that. And I want you to trust me. Please let me listen to what's troubling you."

Melissa glared at her, then stood up and faced her squarely, "Okay, *fine*. Wanita is having an abortion, and she and Bill are going to Mexico to forget. Are you satisfied?" She yanked the towel off her head, threw it on a chair, then sped through the house, thrust the screen door open and stood outside, hands on her hips, her back to the house. The door slammed and bounced shut.

Vellie stood there staring at her. She turned back to the sink, neatly stacked some of the dirty dishes, and took the pie out of the oven. Then she put the hand towel through a drawer handle.

Outside Melissa breathed in the damp air of a coming storm. She could barely smell the scent of horse-flesh from the Timmermanns'. She looked toward their farm as far as she could see, as if by looking hard at the horizon, the edge of the earth, she might somehow dissolve into a thin, pale, painless wisp of cloud and float out of reach.

She closed her eyes and let the hot tears squeeze from their resting place to meander down her cheeks. Wrapping her arms around herself, she let her head drop as she sobbed.

Inside, Vellie squeezed the hand towel for courage. Then she walked slowly to the door so as not to startle Melissa from her thoughts. "Sometimes a long hard ride is all there is to do," she said softly through the screen. She waited just a moment. "Shall we saddle up?"

Without a word, Melissa headed straight for the barn to get a bridle. Vellie followed her.

They rode a full run across the meadow and down along the creek. Melissa was in front, blinded by involuntary tears—both from the wind whipping into her eyes and the pain she had finally begun to express.

She rode nearly wrapped over the back of her horse, fingers fisting the reins with Sassy's mane. She had chosen the bareback saddle so she could feel as one with the horse as possible.

The rhythm of hooves hitting earth numbed the noise in her brain. Noise that condemned her. She urged Sassy on to ride faster. She thought of Pegasus. She closed her eyes and imagined she was riding Pegasus. His wings spread wide and they lifted from the ground. The solid, heavy raising and lowering of his wings whipped the air.

Nothing matters when you're riding the winged horse. Traveling time and space. Your body wind-whipped. Rhythm piercing your soul.

She could barely breathe. The wind came and went from her lungs with the pounding of hooves and dark clouds breaking on one another. But she herself was not breathing.

Eyes still closed, she unclenched her right fist to press her palm against the soft furriness under Sassy's mane. Hot from riding hard, Sassy's coat began to stick to Melissa's hand as she held it there.

"Look out!" was the last thing she heard before she felt her body break.

ELEVEN

Vellie listened closely to the doctor, but never took her arm away from across Melissa's body. The dark clouds outside made it seem later than it was. A thin candle lamp by the bed was the only light in the room. The goldness of it lit Melissa's pale face and also managed to reach Vellie's face as well as the doctor's who was standing on the opposite side of the bed. As he spoke, the shadow behind him seemed to grow with a life of its own, mocking his every gesture.

"She is to move around as little as possible. She's sleeping soundly—I gave her a sedative so she won't wake up for, oh, could be tomorrow before she comes around. But don't worry. As you know, the sleep is letting her body recover without any disturbance. She was very lucky to hit the water and not those rocks."

Vellie had turned to look at Melissa. She looked so much more like a child in deep sleep—her face so tiny with the oversized bandage over most of the left side, her eye and cheek and ear. Two fingers broken, her shoulder badly scraped. Her legs were bruised and cut up, but not broken.

"Thank you, Doctor. I'll see you to the door."

"Don't be silly, Vellie. You stay with your patient. I remember the way out." He smiled kindly and patted her shoulder like a father. "My prescription to you, my dear, is don't blame yourself. Kids fall off horses all the time. You know that. She's going to be fine." He leaned affectionately and whispered, "She's got the best mother in these parts looking after her."

Vellie smiled up at him and squeezed his hand still on her shoulder. "Thank you," she whispered. And then he was gone.

The quiet of the afternoon was like a shroud around Vellie. Melissa was sleeping peacefully, the sound of her breathing deep in rest. The storm had come and gone quickly, though there remained a drizzle enough to dampen the window pane.

How stupid to suggest a hard ride when the child had only been riding for a few days! Vellie thought. But she was glad she'd at least gone with her.

She sat for a long time just looking at Melissa's face. Resting. So young. Like Michael's. She took a deep breath, remembering back years ago to the night of his accident. She had just turned the radio on for the news to keep her company while she made dinner. None of the kids were home. But they would be. It was Sunday night. And then the phone rang. The voice asked her to come immediately to the hospital; her son had had a terrible accident and they needed her signature for some papers or something. She really didn't hear the words that followed "accident."

When she got there, he lay limp. Tubes everywhere. Meaningless to her. They seemed to hold him prisoner. The doctor had pulled a chair up close for her to sit near him. He told her the boy was in a coma but that she should talk to him. He might be able to hear her . . .

She sat there for days, holding his hand. Rubbing it in hers. Holding it and idly tracing unshaped figures across the knuckles and along the veins. She matched the size to hers. He had grown so—like a colt—all legs. And his arms seemed too long. His hands broad and strong. All the time she talked and sang little songs she made up.

Then she had gotten angry. He was much too young and strong to die, she told him. How could she live without him? He was her baby.

And now, as she sat by Melissa's little body, holding her hand, smoothing her hair, her throat began to dry; she couldn't swallow for the pain of something like a rock stuck there. She leaned forward and, as she kissed Melissa's forehead, the tears rushed through her like a train. She stayed there, holding Melissa's hand between hers, elbows on the bed, her forehead resting on the tightly woven fingers of three hands, and wept.

"God," her voice shook as she struggled quietly for words, her eyes squeezed shut, impressing colors in her mind. But there were no words. Only tears. And the dawning awareness of God's presence, like the warm and golden glow from the candle lamp. The rock inside her throat diminished. And her soul felt at once exhausted and resting.

She kept Melissa's hand knotted in hers while she looked around the room. It had been Michael's and Mark's room. It had long since lost the flavor of their childhood and teenage years. She had kept the room as Mark's while he was in college. But when he graduated and moved to the city, taking everything with him, she had had the room redone as a guest room. Lighter fabrics and nicely framed prints replaced posters.

"Thank you, Father," she prayed, still taking in the past and present of the room, "for my children."

Vellie tucked the sheets around Melissa's shoulders, though she hadn't even twitched since she was first put to bed. Vellie kissed her forehead, whispered good-night, and went to her own bed. As Vellie walked back into her room, her reflection in the dresser mirror caught her eye. She drew closer, her gaze locked on the tired eyes of her image. She folded her arms and leaned across the top of the dresser, resting her chin on her wrist. Then she quietly, tenderly whispered to herself, "There will be no grandchild." She breathed heavily with pain, becoming fully aware that her first grandchild was being put to death at the hands of his or her parents. And there was nothing she could do to stop it.

Oddly, an old lullaby came to mind and she mouthed the words, the tune rolling through her mind with the dark images she had never really noticed before: "Rock-a-bye baby in the treetops. When the wind blows, the cradle will rock. When the bough breaks, the cradle will fall. And down will come baby, cradle and all."

* * *

The next morning, as the hours passed, Vellie sang to Melissa from time to time. She'd leave to do a chore or visit Jasper on the porch and then sit with Melissa and sing softly. Sometimes she even made up a tune and words.

> Whisper sweet morning rain
> On our roof up above
> Gently remind us
> To fill our hearts with love
> Scatter grey and lonely clouds
> Let the morning sun shine through
> Give us life for a new day
> To do all the things we need to do
> Sleep softly little one
> Let me hold you as you cry
> Wake as when the sun breaks through
> And know the joy you bring to life.

✻ ✻ ✻

When Melissa woke up that afternoon, her body ached tremendously, like thousands of bony knuckles rolling over her. Vellie had opened the window earlier and the sun proudly flooded the room. Melissa opened her eyes slowly, shading them from the piercing brightness. Vellie came in with a glass of ice water.

"Hey Missy, where ya been?" Vellie asked playfully, hiding the wash of relief that poured through her body like a fresh spring.

"I don't know," Melissa answered, reaching with her good hand to touch the bandage over her face.

"Be careful, darlin'. Doctor's not changing that bandage till tonight."

"What happened?"

"You don't remember?"

"Hmm mmm."

"Think a minute. What was the last thing you remember?" She put the glass by the bed then sat on the edge.

Melissa rubbed the top of her head and closed her eyes tight. "I think," she started slowly, "I think I was flying on Sassy's back. I remember I could feel her coat hot and sticky on my hand."

"Is that all you remember?"

"I think so."

"You don't remember the creek?"

"I remember you shouting something and then I felt something break."

"That's about the size of it. I brought you some cold water. You thirsty?"

"Yes." Melissa tried to sit up but the pain throughout her body forced her to groan and lie back.

"Ouch," Vellie said. "Here, let me help you. You just relax." Vellie managed to get her arm under Melissa's head and pillow. With her knee and thigh wedged under, Vellie managed to hold Melissa cradle-like and tip the glass of water for her to drink.

The cool, wet glass against her bottom lip felt like a bit of life to Melissa. She sipped the water weakly but greedily and then indicated she was finished.

"Are you hungry? I've got eggs just begging to get scrambled." She eased Melissa back.

Melissa smiled at the image. "Sounds great."

"Perfect." Vellie almost glided to the door. "Be back in two shakes of a lamb's tail."

"Vellie," Melissa said weakly, but Vellie heard her and turned.

"Yes, Miss?"

Melissa had her eyes closed and was biting her upper lip, trying to hold back tears.

Vellie came and sat back down on the edge of the bed. She swept Melissa's hair back tight off her face with the weight and breadth of her hand.

"Never mind." Melissa tried to turn away, the tears coming to her eyes. One escaped down her cheek, but Vellie wiped it back into her hair. Then Vellie kissed her gently on the forehead and went on her way to the kitchen.

TWELVE

It was several days before Melissa could get out of bed comfortably, other than trips to the bathroom.

Vellie insisted she do the muscle-stretching exercises the doctor had suggested to keep her legs and back from getting stiff.

✳ ✳ ✳

One afternoon while Melissa was resting, Vellie came in. "Are you sleeping?"

"No." Melissa smiled and stretched carefully.

"I thought it was about time we had a serious talk."

"I know. I should never have ridden Sassy so hard. And I'll never ride again with my eyes closed. I just figured she'd keep running on. I never dreamed she'd take a jump."

"And she had no idea your eyes were closed." They laughed together. Then Vellie got a little more serious again, her voice gentle. "That's not really what I wanted to discuss with you. You know that."

Melissa bit on her upper lip.

"I want to talk to you about our discussion—before the accident."

"I know. I wondered how long it'd be before you brought it up." There was a pause and Melissa fidgeted with the sheets. "I don't think I can talk about it."

Vellie sat on the edge of the bed and leaned sideways over her, propped on her hand. "I know, honey. I don't want to hurt you." She stopped. "I'm sorry. I shouldn't push you like this. It's just that—you see—I care about you and I think if you'd talk about it maybe it would help. But I'm wrong to push you so hard. So you get some rest," she patted Melissa's arm, "and I'll be downstairs doing . . . something."

Melissa smiled, amused. "Vellie, thank you. It means a lot to me, you know. I just can't talk about it."

Vellie forced a smile, nodded, and left the room.

Outside she shouted for Jasper, who came at a fast waddle. "Jasper! I need a walk. You up to it? Good!" And off they went down the path.

Vellie shook her head at herself as she walked. Her thoughts flipped between Bill, the grandbaby, and Melissa without any hesitation, as if they were all one thought. One pain.

"How far do you butt into someone's life?" she asked herself. She and Post had always tried to balance allowing the children to make decisions, along with making decisions for them. Even when it was a decision whether or not to talk.

What she thought was rather ironic was that, even though Bill had been a decision-making adult for years now, he was making a decision she had no part in. And yet it had everything to do with her. And with the life of a human being who also had no part in the decision. This would have been her grandchild. Her first-born's first born. *He doesn't even see it as death! If Melissa at fourteen can see so clearly that this is a death, a loss, then why is it so difficult for someone at 32? Or any age?*

❋ ❋ ❋

Melissa sat by the window and watched them walk down the trail. Something like a wad of tape swelled in her throat and tears spilled over and down her cheeks as she blinked. She let them fall.

She turned from the window, wiped her face, and slowly headed downstairs. Even in Vellie's absence, the house was absolutely resonant with her presence. Her warmth, her humor, her kindness were in every color, every piece of furniture. Melissa went to Vellie's desk and pulled out the chair and sat down. To the casual eye, the stacks of papers and correspondence seemed out of order. But Melissa knew Vellie had them organized into her own system. And the family pictures on the desk, the ledge, shelves, and all about the house, were not randomly placed. They were placed exactly where Vellie wanted them to be.

On the bottom shelf of the bookcase to Melissa's left was a short stack of picture albums. She lowered herself to the floor where she could open one up. There were pictures of Vellie and Post on their honeymoon. Then their first anniversary—a trip to Niagara Falls. And then Bill as a baby. Post as a proud and radiant father. Pants two sizes too big, held up by an awkward belt. Cheek to cheek with his first-born. It occured to Melissa that Bill would not be able to hold up his first-born. She wondered if the baby would have looked like that. Fat-cheeked, with fuzz for hair. Nope. Probably a head full of hair, after Mama. More olive-skin-toned.

Melissa closed the book and replaced it on its shelf, brushing the dust from her fingers, and watched the sunlight on the carpet slowly move as time passed. She felt nothing. Just still, quite still. No pain. No ache. No thought. She stared at the sunlight as if in a trance. The color seemed to drain from everything around her. No sound. Just a taste of something like dust in her mouth. Swollen and heavy inside, the dust seemed to be the very stuff she was made of. She watched little particles of dust dance in the rays of sun above the desk until she could no longer see them.

THIRTEEN

The Fourth of July came in the middle of a soggy week but it seemed to every year. Melissa was almost completely back to her old self and was helping again with the chores. She wasn't riding as much or nearly as hard. Tim thought it best to work back slowly. And with the weather like it was, there wasn't much left to practical argument.

Vellie was planning a picnic and had invited Tim and his family to join them at the high-school football field later that afternoon. Melissa helped with making the sandwiches and potato salad. She jabbed peanut butter into celery sticks, made deviled eggs, all the while trying to picture what it would be like to be a student in

Vellie's class as she listened to Vellie describe the school and how the fireworks are done each year.

Finally they were all packed up and ready to go.

The high school was about four stories high and on an incline. The football field behind it was fenced in but all the main gates were open for people to be able to get in easily. Giant red, white, and blue helium balloons would soon be tied to the top bleachers. The field still smelled freshly cut from early that morning. It had rained off and on, keeping it from being unbearably hot. Vellie couldn't remember a Fourth of July when it hadn't been raining.

Tim brought heavy canvas to cover the ground so they wouldn't be sitting in mud or swampy grass. Then he and Sammy spread a thick rug-like blanket for them to sit on. Another canvas, rolled, lined the side for a quick cover over them if it should start to rain again.

Others were arriving, too, and setting up their picnics. Vellie and Melissa began to set places for everyone and take out the containers of food. Tim and Sammy disappeared to throw the frisbee. Tracie hadn't arrived yet.

As various people passed, most knew and greeted Vellie. Two girls in their early twenties stopped by and Vellie introduced them to Melissa. They were former students from years ago. She introduced Melissa as a friend visiting from out of town. The students chatted with them a bit and soon went on their way.

Melissa watched Vellie continue to get supper ready for everyone. *A friend . . . from out of town*. Most grown-ups would have told more in order to put things into perspective. She liked what Vellie told them. It made her feel safe. Like it was nobody's business who she was or why she was there. She smiled.

Vellie glanced up. "What?"

"Nothing."

"Darlin', will you go find Tim and Sammy and tell them to get here fast? Supper's ready."

"Sure." It took her only a minute to find them throwing the frisbee in the end zone under the scoreboard.

Tracie had arrived when they returned to Vellie. They ate to the sounds of barbershop quartets, bagpipes, square dancing, clogging, and other talents performing on the shell stage. The field quickly filled up with families and pets. Children ran on the grass between blankets like rats through a maze. The air was also full of summer aromas—barbecue, melons, freshly cut grass. Occasionally, the smell of garbage wafted across the field.

Every once in awhile an obligatory bee came to threaten territorial rights on whatever was not being watched at the moment. But, for the most part, the town had done well to eliminate the flying and crawling creatures of summer.

After supper, Vellie initiated a word game in which Sammy became the winner with great ease.

It didn't get dark until after 9:30, and the gibbous moon was bright through the shifting clouds. Then the fireworks raced and screamed across the sky. They all lay on their backs and the colorful explosions seemed just over their heads—almost like they could reach out and grab a burst. Whistles and explosions and colors lasted only twenty minutes. And then came the grand finale with the loudest booms and rockets, seven and eight bursts simultaneously lighting the sky to the sound of "Oh, Say, Can You See" trumpeting from musicians on the stage. The scoreboard lit up, rigged with lights to be the American flag. People all across the field lit sparklers and waved them as they sang.

When it was all over, people clapped and cheered. Then, as if in retaliation for the somewhat violent attack on an otherwise quiet evening, it began to rain. Everyone scurried to pack up, grab blankets and canvas, and run to their cars and trucks.

Tim dropped Vellie and Melissa off before taking his family home. Jasper was glad to see them but stayed on the porch. Lightning lit up the porch just as the suburban headed toward Timmermanns'. The thunder followed in a rumble. The storm itself wasn't very close.

"Why don't you change out of those wet clothes and meet me back out here in ten minutes?" Vellie asked as they peeled off their rain ponchos. Melissa wore Michael's bright green one because she didn't have anything. Vellie hadn't mentioned who it belonged to; she simply happened to pull it out of the back of the closet where she'd gotten her own.

"Aren't you going to change, too?"

"Yes, of course." Vellie hung the ponchos over the railing where they wouldn't be in the path of the windy rain. "But I have something to tend to first."

Inside it was dark. Melissa flipped a light switch but there was no light. "Power's gone out," she called to Vellie as she came in.

"No problem. We'll just have milk instead of hot chocolate." Vellie smiled. "The backup generator should kick in soon. It'll give electricity at about fifty percent. That'll keep the freezer and refrigerator from thawing stuff out. We'll just have to use candlelight." She made her way to the kitchen as if it were sunlit, opened a drawer by the stove and pulled out two boxes of matches. Then she went to the pantry where she kept a box full of candles on the floor under the bottom shelf. She took six out.

She grabbed the kerosene lamp off the bottom shelf and lit it first. She put it down on the kitchen table and turned the wick up to give off lots of light. Then she got two candles off the mantel in the family room and lit one for Melissa.

"Here you go. Take that upstairs with you. Oh, and take this candle, too. When you get to your room, leave this one lit by your bed and you can use the other candle to get around with. Here's a box of matches for you to keep."

"Okay," Melissa said, gazing into the flame and then carefully ascending the stairs so as not to let it go out.

Vellie went over to the refrigerator. When she opened the door, the light inside came on. The generator was working. She took out the apple pie and set it on the table. She poured two glasses of milk. Then she ran upstairs to change clothes—unlit candle in one hand, matches in the other.

A few minutes later, Melissa came down. Vellie hadn't come down yet. The only light was from the oil lamp. She blew out her candle and went to the oil lamp. She took it and the pie and milk, on a tray, out to the porch table. She had to make another trip for plates, serving knife, and forks. Then Vellie joined her.

"Last year we didn't get fireworks," Vellie said, cutting a slice of pie for Melissa. "Completely rained out. Just like this, only it started the night before and saturated the field and kept on raining. At least it was only misty till this afternoon."

"We got rained out in the city, too." Melissa began to eat her pie. Vellie turned the wick down as low as it would go without putting out the flame. "It was great tonight, though," Melissa added. "At home a bunch of us kids used to go up to the top floor of our building, climb the little ladder that goes up to the hatch-like door, and go out on the roof. Some big bank or something set fireworks off their building every year and you could see them real good from just about anywhere in town. We thought it was great. But they weren't anything like tonight. I've never seen fireworks so close. And all the people singing and stuff."

"It is rather wonderful to be in such a crowd and have everyone suddenly be friends for the length of a song. Sharing love for your country. Feels good, doesn't it?"

Melissa nodded, watching the rain. "I think it's also very lonely."

Vellie cocked her head, asking why without saying the word.

Melissa glanced at her and answered, "I was looking around at all those faces. Everyone was glowing in
the light of those firecrackers and lights and sparklers.
I was carried away, too, just like everyone. Singing and
yelling. Then when I looked around at those faces I
thought, I don't know these people. I don't know anyone.
And none of them know me. If I hadn't come, no one
would have known the difference."

She looked at Vellie for a moment, debating
whether or not to continue with what she thought. "Even
you," she finally said. "I looked at you and you leaned
over and, I don't know, grabbed my shoulder or something while you sang. You were really enjoying yourself.
But I thought, I don't know you. And you don't know me.
And it felt cold inside. Like a basement garage. But there
was something else, though. I can't quite figure it out."

As Vellie listened, it was almost as if she heard her
own memories echo similar feelings. She remembered
how lonely she had been at her oldest sister's wedding.
Vellie was not quite fifteen then. Everyone around her
was laughing, and there was dancing out on the lawn.
Her sister was married at the country club and all the
"right" people were there for this most festive occasion
of the mayor's daughter's wedding. The food was excel-
lent and the wedding was beautiful. But Vellie had felt
lost—even though she knew everyone, in the sense that
everyone in a small town knows everyone else. And that's
what felt so odd to her. For the first time she felt like a
stranger. She didn't know her sister or the man she was
marrying. She didn't know her father who was roaring

with laughter and engaging anyone in a jovial "intimate" conversation. She didn't know her mother, so warm and personal with each person who congratulated her. Vellie had wandered off by herself after a reasonable time of shaking hands and being friendly. It was an early evening in September and the moon was barely a sliver. It was the day before new moon when it would be all dark. She decided then that *that* must be how the moon felt on new moon. Completely shaded from the earth . . . cold and dark . . . unseen and unknown.

Vellie turned and saw Melissa again. "I guess it's like the moon at new moon. Hidden from the sun. When there's no light to reflect, it does get cold and dark. And lonely."

"Yeah," Melissa whispered, nodding. "That's exactly it."

"Once you start to know somebody and care for them . . . well, maybe then it's like reflecting the sun. You begin to reflect a sort of light to that person."

Melissa nodded her head. The rain had subsided a bit and there was actually a slight chill when the wind came. Vellie finished her last bite of pie and leaned back in her chair. "Mmmm, I just love apple pie on a stormy summer night."

"Even when it's cold?"

"Even when it's cold."

"Do you think it's possible to lose the ability to reflect light?"

Vellie looked at Melissa for a moment, her arms still straight out, wedged between her shoulders and the table. Then she breathed a sigh and let them bend again. "You sure like to stick to a subject."

"I'm sorry," Melissa said shyly.

"No, no. That's okay. Let's see . . . Repeat the question."

"Once you love someone, and then maybe you don't anymore . . . is it possible to stop seeing your love reflected in them? Or will they stop seeing it reflected in you?"

"Oh, darlin'. I'm not sure I really understand what you're asking. Let me ask you this. We just said a moment ago there must be light in order to reflect it. So does the person you're thinking about still give off light enough for you to reflect?"

Melissa shook her head slowly.

"In a relationship, I think," Vellie continued, "whatever is being given by one person is reflected in the other. Good or bad. And that's true for both people. It may not seem that way, because of the way the light is received, or interpreted. Like in *Till We Have Faces*. Orual cannot reflect the true love of her sister Psyche because of her own jealousy, right? Therefore the reflection, or the way in which she tries to love Psyche, becomes one of betrayal rather than reciprocated love equal to Psyche's love."

Melissa picked up the analysis. "And then Psyche realizes her sister's love is not the pure love she always thought it was." Melissa thought for a moment. "I also think Orual saw reflected in Psyche the eternal pain of knowing her own loneliness and inability to love."

"The whole thing's quite a story," Vellie said.

"It's so much more complicated than that, too. How it all winds up, I mean. Do you think it's all true? I mean, that we're all part of each other? That we move in and out of each other and the decisions we make and feelings we feel?"

"I think that's very true. It's a step further in from the idea of reflection. We can only reflect another person when we truly take them inside. Even if what we take inside is a misunderstanding of the other person. Like in Orual and Psyche's case. I think living in and out of each other means knowing that we are greatly affected by each other's lives and decisions. Even by just the other's presence."

"Nobody understands that, do they?"

Vellie didn't respond; she waited.

Melissa continued, "If they did, a lot of things would be different."

"Well," Vellie began carefully, "I think it's important to think about why there is a misunderstanding between you and this person you're thinking of. On the other hand, the answers may not lend themselves to words, you know."

"Words aren't everything, are they?"

"No." Vellie sensed a switching of gears in Melissa's illustration. "But sometimes it seems they're the only thing. And so we try to force more meaning into them than they were meant to have. But meaning spills out from the words into the feelings, the touches, the living that we do. So what we say will be held accountable by what we do. And it's in the doing and the saying, which become the living, that we move in and out of each other."

Melissa nodded, frowning in deep thought.

"Time to turn in?"

"Yes," Melissa said, rising.

FOURTEEN

Vellie woke with a start, not sure what woke her. She sat up, but all was silent. Then another shout chilled through her—from Melissa's room.

She ran in and Melissa was sitting up in bed rocking, holding her arms across her middle. She shouted again—but it was actually a loud, deep sob. Vellie rushed to her and enfolded her. She was shaking and sobbing in long, loud, heart-wrenching sobs. Vellie rocked with her, smoothing her hair back, and then holding her. "Darlin', what is it? Shhhhh, you're okay darlin', it's just a bad dream. Please wake up, honey. You're okay, Mama's right here."

"No!" Melissa screamed and tried to pull away, apparently still dreaming but responding to the conversation. "You're not here!" Her eyes were open but it was obvious she wasn't really seeing.

"I am, honey. I'm right here."

"You lie!" She stood up in the bed, worked her legs and feet up and down, then stepped off backwards and walked until she backed into the wall. "You're not here and I'm dead."

Vellie tried to play along with her. "Okay, darlin', I'm not here. Why are you dead?"

"Don't call me darlin'! *You* are not allowed to call me darlin'. You hear me?"

"Okay, I'm sorry. Why are you dead?"

"Because you killed me. You killed me!" She threw her arms around herself and started turning in circles, whimpering. Vellie wanted to go to her, but she was afraid of what Melissa might do.

"Melissa, if you're dead, how come I can see you? And hear you? How can you be talking?"

She slowed a minute and then slid down the wall into a crouch. "Because you left me here to live," she said more quietly but still in a high pitch.

Vellie came around the bed and crouched to her level. "Then that means you're still alive, doesn't it?"

"No!" she shook her head, breathing with jerks, "No. No. *No.* Why didn't you want me? Why didn't you kill me?"

This sounded strange but Vellie tried to play the part to draw Melissa out further. "Because I did want you . . . that's why you're here, alive."

"I should be dead. You didn't really want me."

"How do you know, dar—Melissa?"

"Because that's what you told Bill, so don't try to lie to me."

Bill? Vellie thought. Now she was really confused. But she decided Melissa had been through enough and it was time to calm her back to sleep.

"You must be very tired, aren't you, Melissa?"

"Yes," she whispered, nodding her head along with Vellie's. "May I help you back into bed?"

Melissa's chin quivered but she pushed herself back up the wall until she was standing again. "I can do it myself."

"I can see you can. You're doing just fine." She straightened Melissa's covers, then pulled them back for her.

"Don't tuck me in."

"Okay, you can do that, too."

"Go away."

"I'm going." She backed around the bed and up to the door and watched Melissa sink back into the covers and fall asleep. She watched for a moment and then went over and pulled the covers up to her chin and kissed her on the temple.

✳ ✳ ✳

For days Melissa seemed quiet and inside herself. She spoke to Vellie only to communicate her plans for the day or to politely greet her.

Vellie watched her closely. The nightmares continued, but were not as demonstrative as that one night. She wondered if Melissa remembered anything from them. They hadn't discussed them. It seemed sometimes Melissa was embarrassed about something—the nightmares?—yet she hadn't verbalized her feelings. And Vellie thought it best not to bring it up.

Yet to Vellie, those times with Melissa had become special. She would come into the darkened room when she heard Melissa crying out, and enfold the shivering bundle and rock her. She would hold her and comfort her like she knew Melissa's mother didn't.

Vellie's own mother had been a strong and quiet woman. Yet she loved her children and held them, touched them. And she disciplined them to have respect for themselves as well as for others. Vellie wondered how Melissa had gained such a sense of herself without that. And yet Melissa's anger often seemed just below the surface. Vellie wondered if she were getting through to Melissa at all.

Vellie came out on the porch with two glasses of iced tea one evening to where Melissa was sitting and reading in the rocker. When she saw Vellie come through the door, she started to get up.

"Where're you going?" Vellie asked lightly.

"Just moving to another chair."

"Don't be silly. You stay where you are."

"But it's your rocker."

"Not at the moment. You're sitting in it. That makes it your rocker. I brought some tea out for you." Vellie pulled her chair up closer to the table and slid a glass across to Melissa.

"Thank you." She took the glass with her injured hand. Her fingers were still on splints but not wrapped as heavily or to her wrist as before. "I'll be glad to get these off my hand. The doctor said another two weeks should do it."

"That will be nice," Vellie said, leaning back in her chair and stretching her legs under the table.

"Why don't you take the rocking chair? You'd be more comfortable," Melissa offered.

Vellie smiled. "No thank you darlin'. I'm fine where I am. Really."

Melissa looked over toward the other end of the porch where hooks were screwed into the ceiling. "Too bad you don't have that porch swing anymore."

Vellie looked at the hooks, too, but didn't reply. She wished she'd taken them down when she took down the swing.

Melissa turned to Vellie. "I said—"

"I heard you," Vellie said directly but quietly, still looking up at the ceiling.

Melissa searched Vellie's face. She didn't recognize the expression. "Is something wrong, Miss Vellie?"

Vellie looked at Melissa like a stranger, but slowly came back. "I'm sorry. No, nothing's wrong. It's just been a long time—" Her voice trailed off. "So what are you reading?" She forced energy into the question.

"To Kill A Mockingbird." She flipped the book so Vellie could see the cover. "I'm going to have to read it next year anyway so I thought I'd get a head start."

"Good for you," Vellie said, nodding. The sun had become a bright red fist on the deepening horizon. Post used to tell the kids that's why they had red clay in the ground, because the bright red fist came down every night and pounded it.

"Miss Vellie," Melissa interrupted gently.

"Mmmmm?" Vellie acknowledged.

"You don't have to come to my room at night, you know, when I'm not sleeping well. I'll be okay."

"I know. I like checking on you."

"But I feel so stupid." Melissa squirmed a little in the rocker. "I'm not a baby. It's just a bad dream every now and then."

"Honey, you've had one or two nightmares to shame Edgar Allen Poe. I know you're not a baby. I just don't think anyone should have to live through a nightmare alone. It's okay."

"Well, I wish you wouldn't do it." Melissa brushed the opened pages of the book across her hand.

"There *is* a lock on your door."

Melissa looked like she'd been caught stealing. She looked hard at Vellie. Vellie knew Melissa knew she could lock the door. It was obvious, then: Melissa hadn't *wanted* to lock it.

Embarrassed, Melissa mumbled she was ready to go to bed and took the two glasses of melted ice in with her.

FIFTEEN

inally, after days of rain, Melissa woke to sunshine. She dressed quickly, determined to spend the day with Sassy alone.

She drank some juice downstairs but decided to skip eating. Vellie wasn't around. Melissa knew she was out doing some farm chores.

Melissa jogged to Sassy's stall with a carrot for her. She held it in her fist and let Sassy try to grab it with her lips. Once she had it between her front teeth, she lowered her head sharply, trying to take it away from Melissa. The carrot broke with a hollow crunch. Melissa loved the sound of the broad, grinding crunch. Sassy stomped a fly off of her back leg.

When Sassy was ready, she took the other half of the carrot from Melissa and nodded her head up and down while Melissa opened the stall door and tried to take hold of her by the halter. Once she had her in the passageway, she hooked her to the grooming ropes and began to brush her down.

"Hello."

Melissa jumped, dropping the brush. "You scared me, Sammy."

Sammy opened his mouth to say something, then changed his mind. His blond hair was tousled and his jeans and tee shirt were dirty from riding. Melissa hung the brush in its place on the wall of the stall and grabbed the saddle blanket off of the door. "So what are you doing around here?" Melissa asked dryly.

"Actually, I was out riding and wondered if you were riding or wanted to ride," Sammy asked shyly.

"What for?"

"To see if maybe we could ride together."

"I don't think so." Melissa threw the saddle over Sassy and pulled the girth across her belly.

Sammy tucked his fingers in his back pockets. "Look. I don't have a lot of friends. In fact, I don't have any. So I don't know exactly how to make one—"

"Obviously."

"Forget it. Have a nice afternoon." Sammy shuffled out of the barn toward his own horse tied outside. Vellie came around the corner of the house.

"Hello, Sammy," she called.

"Hello, Miss Vellie," he said politely but coldly, mounting.

"Is something wrong?"

"No ma'am, just needin' to get on my way. Excuse me." He spurred his horse and galloped across the open field toward the creek and the far side of his daddy's property.

Vellie came into the barn just as Melissa was buckling Sassy's bridle. "Going for a ride?"

"It's a beautiful afternoon and I want to enjoy it."

"What happened with Sammy?"

"What do you mean?" Melissa mounted Sassy. Vellie came alongside and patted Sassy's neck.

"I mean he seemed a bit . . . embarrassed. Or upset or something."

"He's just weird. I mean, he's ten years old but he acts like he thinks he's twenty or something."

"Melissa, Sammy is old for his age. He's never been around other children. Only his father and the people who work for him. He's really a nice guy and he'd make a good friend."

"I don't want a friend."

"Now *you're* acting ten." Vellie put her hand on her hip.

"Thank you." Melissa sneered. "Please move—I don't want to step on you."

Vellie stepped back and Melissa urged Sassy to go forward.

"Watch your head," Vellie called as Melissa ducked under the barn door.

Melissa breathed a sigh of freedom as she trotted across the field toward the creek. She thought about Sammy. Maybe he wasn't such a bad kid—just a little too polite or something. The first time she met him, he was cooling down one of the horses after training hard all morning. He looked so young, but when he talked he made her forget how old he was. He even seemed older than the boys she knew at school. And that made her feel uneasy; she didn't quite know how to talk to him so she usually sounded like a brat. But he didn't know how to talk to her either.

Besides, she didn't really care how she sounded. Today she wanted to be by herself and ride across the fields and imagine she was a pioneer seeing the land for the first time.

When she got to the creek she saw Sammy's horse tied to a tree and Sammy was on the other side of the creek crouching with his hands in the water. Her shadow fell across him and he looked up. When he saw it was Melissa, he smirked. "First you want to get rid of me, then you follow me?"

"I didn't follow you." She dismounted. "How should I know you were down here?"

Sammy didn't respond; he turned his attention back to the water. Melissa crouched too. "What are you doing?" she asked, sincerely interested.

"What do you care? Why don't you just go away and leave me to my business?" he retorted.

Melissa was quiet for a minute. She realized she had the upper hand and it made her feel less threatened by him. In fact she almost felt sorry for him. "I'm sorry. I was rude and there was really no reason for it."

"Forget it." His tone didn't change.

A few moments passed in silence. Melissa scratched her head trying to think of something to say.

Suddenly Sammy splashed out of the water. In his fist was a fish. He smiled, showing it to Melissa.

"How did you do that?"

"Patience and good reflex. It's how the bears do it." He threw the fish back into the creek, then leaned back on his hands, plunged his bare feet into the water. "I come out here every now and then just to keep limbered up. Usually, though, I stay down yonder on our property where there's a waterfall-like place. That's the best place to catch 'em."

"Why did you throw him back?"

"Why would I keep him? He's just a guppy. Besides—I told you, I do it for the exercise. So why are you here really?"

"I was out riding and saw you sitting there."

"No, I mean here in Muntson for the summer."

Melissa picked up a stick and popped it in half. "Because my mother and her boyfriend decided to take a vacation in Mexico."

"Oh."

A moment of awkward silence passed.

"You're lucky you have a mother *and* a father," said Melissa.

"Yeah right. Life is much easier that way."

Melissa looked at him sideways.

Sammy continued, "You think it makes things better to have two parents? Well I may as well have one. My mother didn't want me."

Melissa went cold and numb inside.

"Shocking, isn't it?" Sammy scratched his foot across a clump of grass.

"Did she tell you that?"

"All the time. Okay, once in a while she'll bring it up when she's especially annoyed with me. But Daddy wanted me. That's all I care about. What about your parents?"

Melissa could feel her insides quivering. She wanted to be very careful about what she said. "I never really knew my father. He was in the military and had to leave us when I was two."

Sammy started to question that but the look on Melissa's face prevented him. "And your mother?"

Melissa took a deep breath. "I don't understand her. And she barely even knows I'm alive. I mean, she's taken good care of me and stuff. But I don't think she likes me very much."

"What about you? Do you like her?"

"Not very much, I guess." Melissa drew circles with her stick in the dirt.

"Do you think all kids feel like that about their parents, or one or the other of them?"

"No."

"That was a quick answer."

"I've given it a lot of thought. If all kids felt like that, then why do they grow up and have kids?"

"Some don't." Sammy sat up and folded his arms across his knees.

Melissa looked at him, wondering if he knew her secret, knowing also that it was impossible.

He added, "My parents wouldn't have, except Daddy wanted a son so much."

Melissa was desperate to change the subject. She could feel a lump grow in her throat and chills grabbed her ribs and her stomach muscles. "So why don't you have any friends?" she tried to ask casually.

"Because I don't know anybody," he answered.

"What about school? There are other kids your age there."

"I don't go to school." He crossed his legs and played with the blades of grass at his ankles. "I'm home-taught by tutors in math, science, literature, the arts, music, geography, history, writing." He sounded like he was reading down a grocery list, tapping his fingers at the mention of each subject.

"Is that why you don't act much like a ten-year-old?"

"I reckon. Then of course there's my father's business. I'm learning good business, how to manage money and people. I'm riding better all the time, too. I really enjoy the work and the animals, but I can't wait to get out of here."

"Me either."

"You? But you're on vacation. Where would you rather be?"

Melissa thought a minute but nothing came to mind.

"Frankly," Sammy continued, "I envy you."

"Why?"

"Living with Miss Vellie. She is the best. She doesn't treat you like a child, you know?"

"No, I don't know."

"She listens. Like it's important to her what you think."

"She can really be nosey sometimes," Melissa said in a sigh.

"How do you mean?"

"I mean she doesn't always mind her own business."

"Look," Sammy said, leaning forward, "I've known Miss Vellie Bagley my whole life and she respects people and their privacy."

"Well she doesn't respect mine."

"Maybe you're confusing nosey with interest."

Melissa shook her head to mean she doubted that.

"You're a very strange girl. You tell me you don't think very much of your mother and it's mostly because she doesn't know you're alive and yet you're upset that someone else does know it and seems to be glad about it. Or at least interested in it. You ought to be a little more grateful for what you've got. You know she was worried sick about you when you fell?"

"I've never heard a boy talk so much."

Sammy was furious. So furious he didn't move for several seconds. Then he got up, waded across the creek, untied his horse from the tree root, mounted him, and rode away toward home.

Melissa sat still, facing the creek and listening to the pounding of his horse's hooves. She broke the stick. The lump in her throat softened into a dull and throbbing ache.

SIXTEEN

As Vellie dug weeds and fingered new life in her garden of snap beans, tomatoes, and the various berries along the little wire fence, her mind was really on Melissa. How could she break through? Ahhh, but that's exactly what she couldn't do. Even after thirty years of teaching, something inside wanted to charge at the problem or at least charge at *getting* to the problem. She knew better. She'd watched it so many times before: The child who is so locked up inside, afraid to trust, vulnerable. She knew she had to wait for Melissa to decide to trust her. But there wasn't a lot of time left to the summer! Still, she knew she couldn't rush her.

She stood up and stretched her back, looking out over all the land. She could see only two neighbors from the garden. Such beautiful lushness to the land. Such peace. Melissa seemed, at least, to be a little more at peace now than when she arrived. When she stopped to think about it, Vellie realized Melissa was in fact beginning to trust her. They seemed to enjoy one another's company.

Vellie took a deep breath and bent back over and began working again. *It's just going to take more time— like growing vegetables,* she thought.

"Hi." Melissa carefully slid off Sassy's back and loosely hung the reins over the fence so he'd have enough room to graze. "Can I do something to help?"

"Hi! Yes, you *may*." Vellie emphasized the word with a smile.

Melissa smirked and rolled her eyes.

"See that wheelbarrow full of weeds? Wheel those varmints to the edge of the woods over there and dump 'em for me. Please."

"Okay." Melissa had to struggle with the wheelbarrow some since she could really only use one hand, but she managed to complete the task.

"Now, that row there needs all the beans picked that look like this." Vellie held up a yet-unpicked bean, a healthy green one with bulges along its sides. "Just snap him off like this and drop him in the bucket. Any questions?"

"Nope." Melissa began to pick. Strands of her hair kept falling, teasing at her face, no matter how often or determined she put it behind her ears.

Vellie watched, chuckled, and pulled a red and white bandana out of her back pocket. "Here darlin'. It's not the cleanest, but it'll do the job for you."

"Thanks." Melissa tied her hair up like a peasant.

"So where've you ridden today?"

"I rode back up to the creek where I fell."

"How did that feel?"

"Well, I don't know if I found the exact place, but close enough. I felt kinda stupid. I shouldn't have fallen off. It wasn't really even a jump."

"It was with your eyes closed."

Melissa smiled and nodded. After a moment she said, without stopping her work, "In a way, I kinda died, didn't I?"

"What do you mean?"

Melissa answered almost too matter-of-factly, "I was unconscious for a long time. I mean, I didn't know I was alive. I didn't know I was dead. I didn't know anything."

Vellie faced her squarely and said pointedly, "I did. I knew you were alive."

Melissa looked at her for a minute. "But I didn't. Until I woke up of course. And it wasn't so bad really. Being dead. It was . . . nice."

"But you weren't dead, Melissa. There's a big difference."

"Is there?"

"Yes." Vellie was grasping for straws, trying to think of something significant to say but she only fumbled with words. "You were resting—revitalizing. That's a different feeling than if you're dead."

"How do you know?"

Vellie stood with her mouth open. Melissa's calm, almost coldness was unnerving, frightening. "Melissa, please get to the point. This verbal ping-pong scares me."

Melissa looked way off at one of the neighbors' houses. "I used to be afraid to die, but I'm not anymore. It's more peaceful than anything else. A peace I've never felt before. In fact, it felt . . . it felt good."

"Melissa." Vellie stepped toward her desperately, but couldn't quite bring herself to touch her. "Why would you want to kill yourself? Suicide isn't an answer."

"Suicide!" Melissa turned, complete shock and surprise on her face. "Who said anything about suicide?"

"Isn't that what you're talking about?"

"No. No. Oh Miss Vellie, I would never do anything like that! When I was nine, my best friend's big brother killed himself—he was sixteen. He filled the tub full of water, got in, and then shot himself in the head. It was so horrible. And it really tore everyone in that family apart. And me, too! That's part of what made me see death as horribly frightening. No, I could never do something like that."

While Melissa had been talking, relief and horror together flowed through Vellie. She sat down in the dirt. Melissa crouched down facing her and placed her hand on Vellie's leg. "Miss Vellie, I'm sorry, I had no idea that's what you were thinking."

"Give me a minute here to breathe and then I hope you will tell me what you *are* talking about."

Melissa resumed picking her beans and Vellie watched her, then said, "I think I'm ready now."

"It's nothing, really. You asked what it felt like, or whatever, and so that's it. I'm not afraid of death anymore. That's all."

"I know it's got to mean more to you than the effect that guy's death had on you."

"No, not necessarily."

Vellie stood up, frustrated, and beat the dirt off the seat of her pants and the back of her legs.

Not noticing Vellie's aggravation, Melissa asked, "How many children do you have?"

"Four—well, three now." Vellie concentrated on picking tomatoes.

"Three? What happened to the fourth?"

"He died in a motorcycle accident." Vellie remembered the hospital room Michael had spent so many weeks in. She'd hardly left it herself. Early one morning, she was awakened, having slept sitting and resting head and shoulders on the bed which had become her habit, when he squeezed her hand. Everything inside her stopped as she watched Michael's face, searched for light, for life. Then his grip lessened as he breathed out his last bit of air. And his pulse stopped.

She sat there. His face looked as it had for days. She reached up to smooth back his hair, but she didn't say a word. Didn't feel anything. The doctor came in and must have said something. She had responded automatically. Finally, she stood up and kissed her boy on the forehead, turned to go, letting his hand gently slip from hers.

Not once had she cried. Not then, not at the funeral, not at the burial. She had simply gone on with her life. With her other children—those of her flesh and those in her classroom.

"Do you miss him?" Melissa asked gently, seeing Vellie had slipped into thought.

"I think about him every day."

"Did you want all your children?"

"Yes, I did." Vellie's eyes searched Melissa's face as she said this.

"My mother didn't want me."

Vellie stopped to think a minute. "Missy, we all go through that with our folks. I did. Especially when I was about your age. And my boys always teased Carol, my only girl, that Daddy found her amongst the corn rows. It's just part of the confusing feelings of growing up."

"That's not what I'm talking about." The look in Melissa's soft brown eyes sent chills through Vellie as she remembered the outburst about the abortion just before the accident.

Melissa, knowing she'd communicated, idly picked a bean and fidgeted with it. Vellie sat back down in the dirt as Melissa began slowly.

"I'm my mother's and father's only child. They have kids by other marriages, but I don't have any brothers or sisters, you know, a hundred percent. When I was about two or three years old, Dad left. Mother said he was in the military and his work took him away. That story worked till I was about seven or eight and had one or two friends who really were 'military brats.' Then I knew she'd lied to me. I guess I really knew all along because I never saw him. I've never laid eyes on my father since I was two years old." Her chin quivered and she took a deep breath and cleared her throat. "I always knew, too, that I didn't really want to know why he left. So I never asked."

She sat cross-legged facing Vellie, still playing with the bean and continued, "About two weeks before I came here, Mother was very sick. I heard her in the morning in the bathroom. She kept telling me it was just the stomach flu, not to worry about it. So I didn't think much about it at the time. But she called in sick at work and she never does that. And she was so nervous all the time and just acted strange for several days. We've never been really close, but I knew something was definitely wrong. I overheard her telling Bill some things and figured out she was pregnant." She looked up at Vellie, suddenly realizing she was talking to Bill's mother. She wasn't sure how Vellie would react.

"What, darlin'?"

She focused on the bean and split it. "I think it's Bill's. And I think he was happy about the baby." She looked for a reaction.

Vellie simply listened. She had already understood it must be Bill's, but long since determined to detach herself from her children's lifestyle choices, as contrary to hers as theirs may be.

"Well," Melissa continued, "It was strange—she wasn't happy about it. The baby, I mean." She snapped the bean in half. "The last day of school I came home early. There was a note for Bill on the table. She'd decided to have an abortion. I took the note to the library and made a copy of it and got the original back to the table and left before anybody got home."

She wiped her hands of the mutilated bean and pinched off a weed, broke it up one segment at a time, and stacked the segments into a pile in front of her.

Vellie consciously put aside her own involvement and emotion to give this child her attention. She leaned forward a little. "What else did the note say, Missy?"

"Nothing . . . it doesn't matter."

Vellie manuevered herself until her knees matched to Melissa's legs and said, "It matters to me, darlin'."

Melissa glanced up but found it hard to look into Vellie's eyes. She was too determined not to cry, too determined not to talk.

The sun had just popped over the tops of the trees, and now it was beating directly down on the little garden. Suddenly it was hot, and the slight breeze of earlier had all but vanished. Melissa pulled the bandanna off her head and combed her fingers through her hair fiercely.

Vellie shaded her eyes, looking up at the edge of the tree tops. "Gosh it's gotten hot all of a sudden." She patted Melissa's legs. "How about you taking Sassy back up and brushing her down? I'll go on back to the house and fix a light lunch. Meet you on the porch in thirty minutes?"

Melissa smiled, relieved at being let off the hook for a moment. "I'll carry the bucket up."

"Can you manage that and Sassy?"

"I think so."

"Great! Thank you." She got up, beating the dirt out of her jeans again and then hollered for Jasper who hurried out of the woods onto the path, watching for Vellie to catch up.

SEVENTEEN

It rained for several days. Summers in the South were like that. Days of scorching, clear sunshine and then a storm would come through for just as many days. Vellie and Melissa were content mostly to sit and read the days away, sometimes together, sometimes separately. One morning Melissa was reading in the family room with the ceiling fan on low. It had brightened up a bit outside, though fog and rain still kept her from leaving the house. So she sat at one end of the sofa, feet propped on the coffee table, and read under the light from the fat blue and white lamp on the end table. There were no ceiling lights in the house except the single bulb in closets and the long fluorescent lights in the kitchen that Post had put up for

Vellie and to her specifications. Melissa liked lamps instead of overhead lights, too. They were cozier. Homier. She felt snug and warm in her corner and circle of light.

Suddenly Melissa heard strange bumping-like noises overhead. She wondered where Vellie was. She put her book down and went upstairs, still hearing scraping and an occasional thud over her head.

The attic door was open like a mouth with its ladder tongue hanging out all the way to the floor, inviting her to be licked up to the noise she heard. She climbed carefully and called out for Vellie. Damp and suffocating heat enveloped her upper body as she stopped on the ladder to look around the grayish glow from the single bulb just above her head.

"Yes, darlin', I'm back here. Am I disturbing you?"

"What *are* you doing?" Melissa asked, emphasizing each word like a parent to a child. Vellie had an enormous box from apparently the deepest, darkest corner of the attic and had dragged it over asbestos and vertical planks of wood, trying to get it to the ladder.

"I thought it would be nice to put the porch swing back out on the porch."

"Let me help you." Melissa grabbed one end with both hands and pulled while Vellie pushed. "This thing is heavy! How did you ever get it this far?"

"Leverage. You don't really have to be strong to move things, just smart. You let things like the floor and those beams help you move it." She demonstrated by lifting one end of the box onto a beam and then twisting the box around so that it moved a full length forward and plunked itself off the beam. "See? And it's solid oak, too. One of the heaviest woods there is." She smiled.

When they maneuvered it to the hole at the ladder, they both got under it on the ladder and eased it down. It took quite a bit of time and effort. When they finally got it safely to the floor and Vellie lifted the ladder and shut the trap, Melissa asked, "Why didn't you just leave it up? Can't these things stay up all year round?"

"Yes, well," she replied, pushing the box down the hallway toward the stairs. It slid easily on the well-worn runner carpet she had over her hardwood floors. "This was Michael's swing. His grandfather made it for him when he was about ten years old. He made it quite thick. Post reinforced the porch roof so it would hold. He said it wasn't too much heavier than normal porch swings but he just wanted to make sure."

"So why did you take it down?"

They stopped for a second at the top of the staircase. Vellie sat down and leaned on the box. "I guess it reminded me too much of Michael. I mean . . . many, many things remind me of Michael. But somehow I couldn't bear to have the swing up. It was like his ghost haunting me. Sometimes at night, I could hear the chain creaking on the hooks when the wind was strong enough to push it. So I had Bill and Tim put it away for me."

"So why are you getting it out now?" Melissa asked quietly.

Vellie smiled warmly and stroked a finger under Melissa's chin. "Because you're here. And I think you'd enjoy reading in it. Come on now," Vellie said as she struggled to get back up, "We've got a long way to go yet."

Melissa got up to help. They eased it down the stairs and slid it out onto the front porch. Vellie went to the kitchen and returned with a razor blade to slice through all the packaging tape.

"What happened?" Melissa asked.

"When?" Vellie continued working.

"To Michael. How did he die?"

"He lost control of his motorcycle out on the highway. He collided with an oncoming vehicle. His girlfriend was riding with him. Somehow she was thrown free. She broke her leg, but recovered okay." Vellie turned the box on its side in order to slide the swing out. The only way she could continue talking was if she continued working. "Michael was in a coma for several weeks. For a while it seemed he was getting better. He even regained consciousness for a little while. But then he—" Her voice trailed as if she couldn't remember something.

"He died, Miss Vellie," Melissa whispered, leaning close.

"Yes." Vellie went to a closet and returned with a dust rag and began to go over the swing, rubbing it mindlessly. "I should never have allowed him to have that thing," she said inaudibly.

"What?"

"He wanted more than anything to have a motorcycle for his sixteenth birthday. I didn't know what to say. I don't like motorcycles. They are monstrously dangerous and I had no earthly idea what to tell him. Post was gone." She spoke slowly and deliberately, as if giving a police report. "He had died two years before that. I talked to Tim and he thought it would be wonderful for him. Said boys Michael's age, especially when they're the youngest in the family, needed something powerful they could control."

Vellie stopped speaking for a moment. Tears surfaced and she refused to have a shaky voice. She continued, clearing her throat, "I allowed my son to have that machine under one condition: that he stay on our property and Tim's and never take it out on the open highway. And he abided by that, as far as I know, for several months. Until that afternoon."

"How long ago was that?"

"Let's see . . . five years ago." She put the rag on the floor. "I should never have let him have that thing."

"Well, he was sixteen. I think he was old enough to handle something like that."

"Obviously not." Vellie's voice was tense. She tried to lift a side up to get up on a chair she'd put outside earlier to stand on, but it was too heavy.

"He was old enough to make his own decisions," Melissa said.

Vellie turned on Melissa with a harshness she didn't recognize. "His own de—I decided whether or not he could have it. *I* decided. *I* was the one who had the final say, not him. I was the one who ki—" Vellie froze bent over, eye to eye with Melissa. She straightened up slowly, then stared at the floor with deep and confused concentration.

Melissa sat very still, watching her. Then she said softly, as gently as the rain was falling, "No, Miss Vellie. It was his decision. *He* decided he wanted it. *He* decided to take it on the highway."

"I know . . . that." Vellie sounded like she couldn't quite remember something important. "I—I thought maybe Post would have allowed him . . . I just wasn't good at being both mother and father."

"But you are a good mother."

Vellie looked at Melissa, denying what she heard but wishing to hear it again.

"At least," Melissa took a deep breath, "at least you wanted your children." She took the box and went through the house to the back door. Vellie dropped the chain to the swing, and stood and watched it rain.

EIGHTEEN

elissa!" Vellie came rushing out of the house, screen door slamming behind her. "Melissa?" She hurried down the stairs, around the house.

Melissa poked her head out of the barn. "I'm in the barn. What's wrong?"

Vellie caught up to her. "Saddle up, darlin'. The Timmermanns' mare is about to drop her foal."

She took the blanket off the door of the stall and threw it over Tavish's back. Then she changed her mind, pulled it off, and grabbed the bareback saddle off the wall and threw it on, skillfully manipulating the straps, still talking. "They just called and invited us to come be part. Oh this is great! Have you ever seen a dam foal?"

Melissa shook her head, also saddling Sassy with a bareback.

"Well it's time you did." She secured the bridle. "There is nothing like watching a new life enter the world. It's beautiful." She stopped a moment, a bit out of breath with excitement. "You about ready?"

"Sure." Melissa buckled the bridle and pulled the reins over Sassy's head. They led the horses out of the barn and mounted. Jasper followed as they galloped off, the distance between dog and horse increasing.

When they arrived, Sammy came running out of the stables. "Miss Vellie! Miss Vellie! Hurry. Ginger's near about dropped her foal!" He grabbed Tavish's bridle.

Vellie and Melissa dismounted and he grabbed Sassy, too. "Thanks, Sammy. Where is she?"

"They're in the stable on the east side. I'll take your horses. Y'all hurry."

They jogged to the stable Sammy had pointed out, hearing Ginger whinny and Tim reassuring her, talking to her like she were a human mother. They came around the corner slowly and stayed outside the stall. Ginger was lying on her side, her head and part of her neck resting on Tim's folded leg. One of his hands was holding her gently by the halter, the other rubbed her neck lovingly. He smiled and waved but kept talking to Ginger. The vet and Tracie had their backs to Vellie and Melissa as they waited; the vet had his hand on Ginger's belly.

"Here she comes, Tracie."

"I'm ready, doctor." She smoothed the little baby's blanket again.

Vellie whispered to Melissa, "Most foals are born right onto the straw, but Tracie always puts out a baby's blanket for her foals."

"I hear you, Evelyn Bagley, making fun of me," she said quietly, without turning to face them. Vellie leaned over and squeezed her shoulder.

Sammy came in and stood next to Vellie. "We have to stay out here, you know," he said to Melissa. "Most mares like their privacy when foaling. But Ginger doesn't foal easily. This time, though, everything seems normal so far."

Ginger grunted and raised her head. Tim let her have the room she needed but kept her from standing, still talking and making little noises at her.

"Here she comes!" the vet said. "She looks good, Tracie. Her head is nicely tucked between those hooves."

Vellie moved aside and guided Melissa in front of her so she could see better. Melissa stared wide-eyed as the foal suddenly seemed to pop out. Tracie wiped the little face and neck.

Before long the foal was completely out and Tim let go of Ginger's head so she could lick her foal clean.

"Did you see that, Melissa?" Sammy was excited, but not too loud. "Wasn't that great? Gosh, there's nothing better than watching a miracle."

Melissa turned and ran out like a shot.

"Melissa?" Vellie called after her.

Tracie stood, wiping her hands in her apron. "What's wrong?" Tracie followed Vellie to the barn door.

Vellie followed Melissa with her eyes, suddenly realizing how painful watching the birth must have been for her Missy. "She'll be okay," Vellie replied, still watching to see where she might end up to be found later. "I'll go after her in a few minutes." She smiled and turned back to the family inside, mustering an air of celebration. "So Sammy, what's her name gonna be?"

"Let's see." He got a serious look on his face as he observed dam and foal together. "I been thinking on it. Seems like she ought to be called Brandy."

"That's a lovely name, darlin'. Listen, will you do me a favor?"

"Sure!"

"Melissa's gone down by the creek a ways and I'm going after her on Tavish. Would you be able to bring Sassy over later, when you get a chance?"

" 'Course. I'll just put her up if you're not home yet."

"Thanks." She patted his cheek and he was off to concentrate on Brandy.

Vellie and Tracie walked to where Tavish and Sassy were put up in the north stables. "I appreciate your call, Tracie. It truly was magnificent to watch Brandy in her first few seconds."

"Mmmm. I thought Melissa would enjoy it, seeing as how she's from the city. I'm sorry it upset her."

"Naw. She'll be just fine. She really takes things in deep inside. That's all it is. You remember being fourteen? Everything is profound." Vellie knew this would appease Tracie's concern and Melissa's privacy would be protected.

NINETEEN

A s Vellie approached the creek she could see Melissa on the other side, downstream, two or three hundred yards away. The trees were thicker on that side and even though evening was close by, and the sun no longer direct, the air remained heavy with heat. She guided Tavish across the creek, then dismounted, leaving him to graze or lap at the water as he chose.

Melissa was crouched beside the water. With stick in hand, she poked chunks of dirt from the bank into the flow. She wiped tears from her face with her other hand but still didn't seem to notice Vellie coming nearer.

"Missy? Darlin', are you okay?"

Melissa nodded her head but didn't look up from her task. Vellie sat down beside her, their shoulders nearly touching.

"Penny for your thoughts." She searched the young, too-serious face. No response. "A tadpole, then," trying to make her smile.

It worked. But the smile faded quickly. "I'm just tired of being confused." A glop of dirt fell into the creek. "She had no right to kill my brother. Or sister."

Vellie leaned over and put her hand into the cool water, watching it braid through her fingers. "I'm afraid every one of us is free to make choices. Even wrong choices."

"She had no right. People say abortion isn't murder, that a fetus isn't alive. But that's not what science says. I've read all about it. I hate her."

"Darlin'." Vellie grimaced, feeling again what it is to hear those words from your child.

"What? You think it's wrong I should hate her? She hates me. She said so. I drove my father out of the house." She stood up, grabbed a younger tree with both hands and shook it. Vellie rose too. Melissa continued shouting, "She should've killed me, too! She should've killed me!" She wept with her forehead against the tree trunk.

Vellie gently took her by the shoulders and peeled her from the tree, turned her and held her close. Melissa buried her face and wrapped her arms around her. Vellie rocked her and stroked her head and back. "Cry, Missy. Cry it all out." She kissed the top of Melissa's head.

After a few minutes, Melissa pulled away and wiped her face. She turned back to the creek and sat down.

"Melissa, how could you be responsible for your father leaving?"

"That's what Mama said in a note to Bill. She said she wouldn't have lost him if she'd aborted me like he wanted."

"Is that what it really said?"

Melissa turned sharply with a piercing look. "You don't believe me?"

"I don't believe you'd lie to me . . . What I mean is, were those really the words she used?"

Melissa looked up and recited the note from memory, accenting the words with vehemence. "It said, *'Dear Bill, I've given this a lot of **thought**, as you asked. I still feel like I'm doing the right thing. I can **barely** keep up with the kids I've already got. I **appreciate** your **concern** and offer to help out, but this is **my** problem. Let me take care of it the way **I** think **best**. I love you. I don't want **this** to come **between** us. And I wouldn't want you to feel **obligated** to me or this **baby** or **resent** me later on if I kept it. It's happened **before**. That's how I lost Carlos—'"*

Melissa dropped her head into her hands and wept. Vellie sat down beside her, shocked. How insane the world had become. She tried to remember what she had recently heard Mother Teresa say. How did it go? Now that people in the United States are permitted to murder their unborn children at will, is there anything left for Americans to destroy? Vellie shook her head. *When did*

137

we stop celebrating the birth of our children? she wondered. She looked at Melissa wiping her face.

"I am so tired of crying," Melissa said.

"It's okay to cry. There's a lot of pain needing to get out."

"It just makes me tired. I don't think it'll ever stop."

Vellie put her arm around her and Melissa leaned against her shoulder. Vellie enclosed her with her other arm, locking fingers. "It won't always hurt this badly."

They were both quiet for a minute. "Sometimes people say things—I'm talking about your mother now—that they don't mean. They can't take responsibility for things or aspects of things and so they put the blame on something or someone who is more vulnerable. What I'm trying to say is that your mother and father had problems before you ever came along. And they would have had them even if you'd never been born."

"How do you know? You don't know them."

"No, but I know people. Unfortunately, your birth was a convenient scapegoat for both of them. I don't mean to hurt your feelings. I just don't want you to blame yourself for their problems. You are much too valuable."

Melissa sat up to see Vellie's face. "Why?"

"Because, Melissa, honey, I believe in life. I believe in *your* life. I believe there is a God and that he knows you and loves you. I believe he created you."

"Then what about—"

"We can't understand that. Right now you and I don't know some things. But God does. And when you believe in him, and focus on him, darlin', it's okay not to know. Because that's what trusting him is all about."

Melissa leaned back on Vellie again. "How can I believe in a God who lets stuff like this happen? How can I believe he cares about me when he doesn't care about that baby?"

"He does care about that baby. I guarantee you, that little life is now with him. You will one day know that little person. I believe that."

"But why did God let all this happen? It hurts so much."

"I know, baby. But I'll tell you something. Without God, you'll spin in the darkness of all that pain. Spin and explode on the inside. But when you go to God with your questions and pain, he will provide comfort and hope."

"I want answers." She pouted.

"I know darlin'. So do I. Maybe we have the answer and we just don't understand it. Or maybe the answer is, 'Wait. Just trust me.' Think of the word 'redeem.' It means, 'To give back.' In this case, 'To give life back.' That's what God is all about. Healing and giving life back. We won't see that completed in this life, as you're finding out. On this earth, there will forever be people who are determined to take life, to destroy it. But God has the power to give back what has been taken away."

"How?"

"One way is through forgiveness—through his Son Jesus. I believe he can forgive your mother. He died for her. More importantly, I believe he came back to life—for her, for you, and for the baby."

"I don't understand."

"That's okay. You will. We can talk about it more later." A few minutes of silence passed. "Let me tell you something else, Melissa. I don't expect you to understand this completely now, but I hope you will remember it. Your mother, whether she knows it right now or not, will replay her decision a million times. And every time she'll hate herself a little more for killing her child. She'll fantasize how it would have been if a thousand things had been different. That's a sort of punishment in itself. And she may never be able to forgive herself entirely."

Then Melissa sat up and Vellie let her go.

"I'm sorry I've messed up your summer." Melissa poked her finger in the dirt.

Vellie smiled. "But my darlin', you have brought joy to me this summer."

Melissa looked perplexed.

"I've learned a lot from you," Vellie continued.

"Like what?"

"Oh," she sighed, "like how we really do affect each other—people in general, I mean. And I'm reminded that no decision is ever made in isolation. The consequences not only impress but enter into lives close to us—and may even touch lives we know nothing about."

Melissa looked at the ground as if digging the earth with her eyes. "I want to have a memorial service." She looked at Vellie who nodded her head, a little surprised. "Tomorrow morning. At sunrise."

"Okay. Why sunrise?"

"I don't know. It's just what came out of my mouth. I guess because sunrise is like hope."

"I agree."

"And a new beginning."

"Mmmm hmmm."

Melissa was silent for a moment, staring into the distance. The crimson sun was half-eaten on the horizon. The sky seemed to grow dark much too quickly. "And I think it will help me," she paused, "maybe forgive my mother."

Vellie smiled slightly, a pained but relieved smile. She took Melissa's hand and squeezed it warmly. "We'd better get back to the house while we can still see."

Tavish had grazed his way close by. Vellie mounted, then helped Melissa mount behind her.

TWENTY

Early the next morning, while it was still dark with a light blue halo on the earth's horizon, they rode together down to the creek. The moon was full and bright behind them; its crisp golden edge foretold the coming of the sun. Melissa filled her pouch with large stones she gathered from the center of the creek. Knee deep in water, she could barely reach each one without her head going under. And the water was cold. Earlier Vellie had tried to talk her out of it but realized the child had to do this her way.

Once her pouch was full and she was out of the creek, Vellie handed her an oversized bath towel. Melissa quickly stripped off all her clothes and put on dry jeans and a sweatshirt she'd brought. Then she neatly laid out her wet clothes on the grass to dry as they continued on their way up through the woods to a clearing Melissa had found.

At the clearing, they dismounted and Melissa handed Vellie Sassy's reins. She took the pouch of stones and went further into the clearing. All around, birds were coming to life as the first light of morning darted horizontal rays through the trees.

Melissa got down on her knees and carefully took each stone out of the bag. They seemed more to her like treasures than like cold, grainy stone. There were five, each a little larger than a brick. As she laid the first stone, she began to speak to her never-to-be-born sibling. "I realize that this seems strange. I'm talking to you like you can hear me. But in a way I think you can." She pulled out the second stone. Behind her, Vellie crouched as well, fingering the leather in her hands.

Melissa completed a sort of triangle with the third stone. The fourth and fifth, she balanced side by side on top. "I think your name should have been Michael, like the great angel of God." She stopped a minute, and then continued, "And like Vellie's son. Because he was wanted."

Vellie felt a shiver go all the way through her.

Melissa continued, "I think you were going to be a boy. Because I think God knew I needed a brother." She took a deep breath and then changed her position to sit cross-legged. She leaned over, her hands curved with all ten fingertips clutching the ground as if to draw courage.

"But I don't know why you didn't get to live. I just want to know why . . ." Her voice trailed and she bit her lip.

Vellie stretched her legs out in front of her, relieving her knee joints from the crouch. Leaning her head back, she opened her eyes onto the clear sky. Tavish nudged at her leg, trying to rip up the grass underneath. She scooted over to oblige.

"Michael, I want you to know I wanted you. Someday I will get to meet you. Vellie said so. But for now I have to let go. I'm really trying hard not to be mad at Mom. I can't help it. I mean, she killed you."

Vellie closed her eyes and couldn't breathe. All these years she had wondered if Post would ever forgive her for Michael's death. Now she realized Post would never have blamed her in the first place. No, it was she who had not forgiven herself. But there was something else. She rubbed a section of leather between her fingers.

"And now I don't get a brother. But you know what? She almost killed me, too. I don't understand. Where do we get the idea parents are supposed to love their children?" She dragged her fingers across the dirt toward herself. "I think most do." She looked at the dirt streaks on her fingertips. "And we're going to be okay." She laid her hands on the stone pile. "I just wanted to say good-bye—and I love you." She bowed her head between her outstretched arms.

Vellie sat up straight and crossed her legs, stiff at this sudden realization: she had not yet forgiven Michael. Here before her, Melissa was acting on her love for a child she didn't know. She was taking the first step to forgive her mother for making a desperate decision that was completely wrong in Melissa's mind. She had much to forgive.

Vellie looked at her palms. She had not known her decision to let Michael have that motorcycle would in fact end in his death. Suddenly great tears flushed down her cheeks. But what she really had to forgive was a son's disobedience to her rather subjective rule. He did not intend to end his life with his decision, yet she had not forgiven him.

She sobbed uncontrollably into her hands. For the first time since Michael's death, she let him go.

Melissa turned and watched Vellie cry for a moment. Then she went to her and sat facing her, their knees nearly touching, like Vellie had done with her in the garden. For a long time they sat together without touching, without interfering in each other's grief.

Then Melissa leaned forward and gently placed her hands on Vellie's shoulders. "Vellie? Let's go home now."

Vellie took a deep breath and drew her face away from her hands and nodded. They helped each other up and hugged.

"It was a beautiful farewell," Vellie said, handing Sassy's reins to Melissa.

"Was it for you, too?" Melissa mounted as did Vellie.

"Yes, I think so."

They rode back down to the creek in silence. The morning was cool, a breeze lilting by occasionally. Melissa gathered her wet clothes and stuffed them in the pouch where the stones had been. Mounted again, they sauntered toward the house, the sun almost full behind it. The moon had begun to fade, almost translucent to the rising sun.

Kimberly M. Ballard lives in Stone Mountain, Georgia. A fun-loving and artistic writer, she enjoys the arts—drama in particular. Her most favorite books include fairy tales, because she loves to watch the good guys triumph over the bad guys.

Like Vellie, Kim is 100% Southern. She shares Vellie's love for her land—and all of nature. And, like Melissa, Kim struggled with life and death issues when she was growing up. Because of her deep, enduring faith in God, Kim is continually challenged with turning her questions into active involvement in pro-life.